"So, what will you tell them?" Jed asked. He took her hands.

She pulled free from his grasp and turned away. "I'm going to tell them I will do whatever is required for the company," she said in a whisper.

"What?" Jed stared at her incredulously. "Why? Surely running Ryan Mining isn't what you really want, is it?"

She smiled up at him. "It's just that—I'm a Ryan. That company has my family's name on it. I'm not going to let my grandmother down—I can't."

Jed nodded silently. He could understand her feelings, even though he didn't approve of what she had decided. "Would you like me to stay and be with you at the meeting?" He slipped his hands gently around her waist.

"Oh, that's sweet of you. But you already took Friday off and you'll be here for me tomorrow. You'd better go back." She pulled him closer. Lightly, she stroked her finger along the hard muscles of his upper arms while dropping her voice to a warm intimate tone. "I want to be back in New York with you as soon as possible. You know that."

"Yes, I know," Jed answered. Wrapping his arms more tightly around her, he lowered his head and gently kissed her. Thoughts of Ryan Mining fled from Caitlin's mind, and all she could concentrate on was being secure in Jed's arms. . . .

# Caitlin

# FOREVER
# AND ALWAYS

Created by
Francine Pascal

Written by
Joanna Campbell

**BANTAM BOOKS**
TORONTO · NEW YORK · LONDON · SYDNEY · AUCKLAND

RL 6, IL age 12 and up

FOREVER AND ALWAYS
*A Bantam Book / March 1988*

*Conceived by Francine Pascal*

*Produced by Cloverdale Press, Inc.,*
*133 Fifth Avenue, New York, NY 10003*

ISBN 0-553-26788-4

*Published simultaneously in the United States and Canada*

PRINTED IN THE UNITED STATES OF AMERICA

O      0 9 8 7 6 5 4 3 2 1

# 1

Caitlin Ryan's clear violet blue eyes sparkled with happiness as she spoke on the phone. "Oh, Jed, our engagement party's a tremendous success already. Almost everyone we invited is here, and they all seem to be having a great time, too." Twisting the phone cord around her finger, she added in a low voice, "All I need to make this day perfect is to have my fiancé here with me."

"I'll be there soon. I promise," Jed Michaels replied.

Curled in a chair in the library at Ryan Acres, Caitlin smiled at Jed's words. She was looking through the french doors to the sweeping back lawn and the pool, where their friends had gathered. Some were splashing around in the pool, while others lounged lazily on the deck. A sumptuous lunch had been set up on linen-covered tables by the caterer.

Jed and Caitlin had told their friends about their engagement a few weeks earlier, but decided to wait until the long Memorial Day weekend to announce it officially. Many of their old friends had been invited to the party, people Jed and Caitlin had known since their days at Highgate Academy, an exclusive prep school, where they had met. Others were from Carleton Hill University, the college from which they both had graduated. There were also friends from New York City, where Jed and Caitlin were now living.

They had moved to New York soon after their graduation from Carleton Hill. Caitlin had found an entry-level job at a weekly news magazine, *National News*, but her talent for writing soon came to the attention of an editor, and before long she was asked to write for the magazine full time. Jed, meanwhile, had studied law at Columbia University, and after receiving his law degree, was snapped up by a well-known firm. His future there looked bright, and Caitlin was sure he would be offered a partnership in a few years.

The day before their engagement party, Caitlin went down to Virginia to Ryan Acres to be there when their friends started arriving.

Unfortunately, Jed had had to stay in New York to finish some work. Now he was calling to let Caitlin know he had just gotten off the plane and was at the airport in Washington, D.C. "So I'll grab a rental car and be there before you know it." His deep voice still held the hint of a western drawl that was a reminder of his Montana childhood.

For an instant Caitlin imagined him standing beside her, his arm around her waist, looking down at her with his incredible green eyes. She smiled, thinking about how lucky she was to be in love with a guy as wonderful as Jed, and to have him love her just as much.

"Just hurry up, okay?" she replied. "I know it's only been a day since we were together, but it seems like ages."

"I know what you mean," Jed agreed in a warm husky tone. "In fact, I've barely been able to keep my mind on the paperwork for that case I'm working on." He chuckled. "Hey, are you sure you wouldn't rather just elope this weekend instead of waiting until the fall to get married? I mean, talk about a long time. Do we really have to wait?"

"Don't you dare tempt me, Jed Michaels," Caitlin said, laughing back. "I just might decide to take you up on that offer."

"Really?" The tone of Jed's voice made Caitlin suspect that he hadn't been teasing.

"Oh, I wish," she answered seriously. "But you know my grandmother would never forgive us if we eloped. Not after all the plans we've made. I mean, we've already reserved the church. And then there are the orchestra for the reception, the white orchids flown in from Hawaii—"

"You've started doing that already?" Jed interrupted, sounding surprised.

"Of course," she replied. "We agreed we wanted a big, formal wedding. Formal weddings take months to plan. Besides," she went on lightly, "think about your sister. You know you wouldn't dare disappoint Melanie. She's already spent hours poring over books and magazines to find the perfect bridesmaids' gowns."

"You're kidding!" Jed cried in a disbelieving tone. "All I can think of is getting through the ceremony without making an idiot of myself. But, then, I guess I'm supposed to be nervous."

"Jed!" she protested. "What an awful thing to say."

"Only kidding," he assured her. "I'm sure I'll love every second of the day, honest." He paused and then added in a low voice, "But what I'm really looking forward to is our honeymoon. All those wonderful days—and nights—alone with you."

4

"Umm," Caitlin responded warmly. Closing her eyes, she pictured them walking on a secluded, romantic beach at sunset.

"Look," Jed said, interrupting her thoughts, "the longer I stand here in this crowded airport, the longer it will be until I get there. I'm going to hang up right now and go get the car."

"Okay. Drive carefully. And, Jed—I love you."

"That goes double for me," Jed said. "Bye."

Slowly, Caitlin hung up the phone. She could hardly believe she and Jed were finally getting married. It was a dream come true. She looked down at the three-and-a-half-carat diamond ring on her finger. When she moved her hand, it winked brightly and made her shiver with delight. It was still new—she had had it only three weeks. She remembered every detail about the night Jed had given it to her.

He had taken her out to dinner at an elegant and intimate restaurant. Each table was set in a private alcove and had a floor-to-ceiling window that looked out on a tiny well-lit garden. Jed had made sure that the centerpiece on their table was an arrangement of Caitlin's favorite flowers—pink roses. Two pink candles in silver holders stood on either side of the flowers, and heavy silver, as well as crystal, sparkled on the linen damask table-cloth.

But what sparkled most was the first course, served to Caitlin alone. Shortly after they had ordered, the waiter set a silver-domed platter before her. Then, instead of lifting the dome as he normally would, he had quietly left. Confused, Caitlin looked over at Jed.

"Why don't you see what's under there?" he had suggested, a nervous smile touching his handsome lips.

Shrugging, she had lifted the dome. There, tucked into the delicate petals of a single pink rose, had been the ring.

"Oh, Jed—" she had whispered. "It's beautiful."

Jed had stood up then and walked around the table. Picking up the ring, he had slipped it gently onto the third finger of her left hand. "Caitlin, will you marry me?" he had asked.

Tears of happiness streaming down her face, Caitlin had managed to nod. Jed then drew her to her feet and pulled her into his arms, kissing her. They had still been wrapped in each other's arms when the waiter arrived with their food. He had smiled, then quietly left to return several minutes later.

Sighing happily at the memory, Caitlin leaned back against the library chair. Could anyone else possibly be as romantic as Jed?

she wondered. Then she immediately answered herself with a smile. *No, of course not.*

Jed's suggestion that they elope was romantic, too. But she truly did want to have a memorable wedding, one she could tell her grandchildren about. And once the day was finally over, she was sure that Jed would agree that she had been right.

And, as she had told Jed, there were other people who would be terribly disappointed if they didn't have a big wedding. Her grandmother and Melanie were counting on it, and so was her father, Dr. Gordon Westlake, who would be giving her away. But Caitlin was doing it for someone else, too—her mother.

Instead of a large traditional bouquet, she planned to carry a small book of poems that had belonged to Laura Ryan as a young girl. Laura was the mother Caitlin had never known. With it she would carry a spray of white baby orchids, trimmed with trailing satin ribbons. At the thought of the woman who had died giving birth to her, Caitlin's eyes filled with tears. She wished that her mother were alive to share her happiness. Caitlin only knew of her mother from the stories her father and grandmother had told her. Dr. Westlake always said how much Caitlin reminded him of her.

The book of poems had been a present from

her mother to her father. She had given it to him just before Regina Ryan had whisked her off to Europe in the hope of breaking them up. Mrs. Ryan had not approved of the poor young medical student, feeling that he was not worthy of her daughter. Once they were in Europe, though, Laura announced to her mother that she was pregnant. Mrs. Ryan kept the pregnancy quiet, assuming that her daughter would give the child up for adoption. But when Laura died, Mrs. Ryan decided to bring Caitlin back to Virginia and raise her herself. It wasn't until Caitlin was a young woman that she was reunited with her father. Now she and her natural father were very close, and he would give her away at the wedding.

He was unable to attend the party that weekend because of a pressing schedule at his hospital. Caitlin knew she would miss him, even though he had insisted that a party like this was for young people and not old doctors.

A quiet knock on the door brought Caitlin out of her reverie. Sitting up and turning to look toward the open door, she smiled when she saw who was standing there. It was Ginny Brookes.

It had been almost a year since she had seen the girl who had been her dearest and closest friend at Highgate.

"Ginny! Hi!" she cried happily as she sprung to her feet. She quickly crossed the room and threw her arms around her old friend. As she did she noticed again how much Ginny had changed from the awkward girl who had always loved horses and ignored her appearance at Highgate. A sophisticated creature had since taken her place. The face Caitlin remembered as being angular now appeared classical with the help of a little skillfully applied makeup. And her mousy brown hair had been highlighted and stylishly cut. "You look positively marvelous," she said honestly.

"You do, too, as usual," Ginny replied with a smile. She stepped back to take Caitlin in. "I can't believe I'm really here, back at Ryan Acres. It's been so long—" She stopped, shaking her head. "Time sure does go fast."

"I know," Caitlin admitted. "Living in New York means being in constant high gear. The time just gets away somehow. And what free time I do have, I spend with Jed."

"Naturally," Ginny agreed. "I know just what you mean. I'm"—she stopped in midsentence, then finished lamely—" uh, busy, too."

"Ginny!" Caitlin said, her eyes widening. "Ginny Brookes, there's someone special. You're seeing a new guy. I can tell. It's written all over your face." Caitlin could barely contain her enthusiasm for her friend. "Who is it? I want details."

But the minute Caitlin said it, Ginny's face changed. A blank and unreadable expression had replaced the earlier glow.

"You're wrong, Caitlin." Ginny shrugged. "I wish there was someone, but there just isn't." Waving her hand in front of her face, she changed the subject. "The plane coming down from Boston didn't have much air-conditioning, and the car I rented at the airport wasn't much better. Would you mind if I went upstairs and changed out of this pants suit?"

"No. No, of course not," Caitlin replied. She was confused by Ginny's reaction to her perfectly innocent question. When they were roommates, Ginny had always been so honest with her. *But, then,* she told herself as she put her arm around her friend's waist and steered her through the open doors into the hall, *that was a long time ago*. They were both adults now, and if Ginny wanted to be secretive about some part of her life, she had every right. Also, Caitlin remembered, they had been estranged for a while because of a boy they had both liked. But that was long over and they were friends again.

"Rollins has probably taken your luggage

up to your room. Why don't you change into a bathing suit, too," she said, indicating her one-piece bathing suit made of shiny aqua material. It was cut high to show off her long, slim legs. Over it she wore a cotton cover-up in a white and aqua print. "Everyone's down at the pool."

"Sounds great," Ginny replied in a happy tone. "Come up with me and we can talk."

"Sure," Caitlin answered, wondering if she had imagined the momentary coolness.

Minutes later she was perched on the edge of the four-poster bed in the guest room Ginny would be using. The maid had not yet had a chance to unpack for her, and Caitlin watched as Ginny unzipped her gray nylon overnight bag. She pulled out the two pieces of a hot pink bikini, tossed them onto a nearby chair, and slipped out of her beige linen pants.

Caitlin was still dying of curiosity about Ginny's new romance and decided to try another approach. "So, besides getting your MBA at Harvard all year and working summers for that investment firm—" She paused. "What's the name again?"

"The Allan Farnes Corporation," Ginny answered, slipping into the bikini bottom.

"Anyway, what else have you been up to? I can't believe you're spending all your evenings curled up with a computer and a spread sheet."

Ginny concentrated on tying her bikini top, and didn't answer right away. She pulled a brush from her purse and ran it quickly through her hair. "Believe me, Caitlin," she said with a shrug, "that really is about it." Reaching into the open suitcase, she took out a lacy white cover-up and slipped her arms into it. "Oh, I do go on dates sometimes, but there's no one special." As if to say the subject was closed, she walked toward the door.

Now really curious about her friend's refusal to talk about her new romance—but positive there was one—Caitlin slipped off the edge of the bed and joined Ginny in the hall.

"I ran into Emily just as I arrived," Ginny said as they went down the broad staircase. She shook her head. "I can't believe how domestic she's gotten since she became Mrs. James Wentworth Kent the Third. Next thing you know, she'll have a bunch of kids hanging on to her skirt."

"I know she'd like that," Caitlin said with a smile.

"Anyway, she said she already knows what she's going to give you as a wedding present. It'll probably be a Cuisinart and a toaster oven and maybe even an espresso maker." Her eyes flew open wide. "Where you're going to put it all is your problem. If the apartment you and Jed plan to live in is anything like mine, you'll never fit half your presents in."

"I know, I know," Caitlin said, laughing. "Emily and Jim are living in a huge old house. Her kitchen alone is larger than my whole apartment." For just a moment Caitlin looked wistful. "You know there are times when I would love to be living that kind of life." She sighed. "I mean, New York is great, but it can be so claustrophobic."

Ginny nodded. "I know what you mean. Sometimes I feel that way about Boston, too."

Coming out of the house, they paused together at the top of the sloping lawn. Ginny searched the crowd below for familiar faces. Since she and Caitlin had gone on to different colleges after graduation, a lot of the guests were strangers to her. "What a crowd!" she remarked. "When you said it was a weekend party, I figured there would be a few guests, but there must be at least fifty people here already. I don't even see anyone I know."

"Sure you do," Caitlin said, assuring her. "Look, there's Brett Perkins and Jill Taylor. And over on the other side of the pool are Roger Wake and Kim Verdi." She grinned. "They're going out now. Can you believe it? Remember when Roger was going with Morgan but he had a thing for Jane? She used to flirt with him madly even though she didn't think she had a chance!"

"Stop!" Ginny laughed. "You're making me feel so old." She shook her head. "Oh, wow. Those were the good old days, weren't they?"

"I don't know," Caitlin said with a smile. "I think I prefer the present."

"Hey, isn't that Laurence Baxter?" Ginny asked, nodding toward the chaise where a handsome young man with a deep tan and dark wavy hair was stretched out. He was wearing a bathing suit, and Ginny could see that he was in great shape.

Caitlin nodded. "And that's Melanie, Jed's sister," she said, referring to the pretty, animated girl who was perched on the edge of a chaise near Laurence. Her head of short, light brown curls was bouncing merrily. She was obviously agreeing with something Laurence had just said to her. "But, then, you know her," Caitlin added.

"Oh, of course," Ginny shaded her eyes with her hand. "I guess I just didn't recognize her at first. But it has been at least a year since I saw her. She's changed, she doesn't look so— girlish as she used to."

"I hadn't really thought about it, but you're absolutely right." Caitlin studied Melanie, suddenly seeing her through new eyes. "She just finished her first year of grad school," she commented. "Maybe that did it."

"That can do it," Ginny agreed knowledgeably. "There's a lot of difference between college and graduate school. You grow up really fast when you realize how stiff the competition in the real world is going to be."

"Umm," Caitlin nodded. She wondered if the difference might just be because Melanie was really happy. She had been through a rough time. When her father, Carl Michaels, had died, she left her home in Montana to move to New York with Jed. She had tried to finish her senior year in college at New York University, but detested it so much she ended up dropping out. Then she got involved with a tough crowd for a while, and it took a long time for her to get herself back on the track. But she had—and finished her undergraduate degree. She had even started working toward her master's degree the previous fall.

Caitlin watched as Melanie laughed at something Laurence had said. She had fixed the two of them up together several years earlier. For a while it looked as though their relationship might have gotten serious, but the romance had quietly fizzled out. With Laurence living in Virginia, and Melanie in New York, the distance was just too great to keep up a relationship.

Caitlin was glad the two were hitting it off now, especially since Laurence's girlfriend was sick with the flu and hadn't come to the party.

That meant he and Melanie were both unattached for the weekend. If they would pair off, it would solve her problem of partners for them for dinner that evening.

"Well," Ginny said, breaking into Caitlin's thoughts, "I do believe I see someone I'd like to latch onto and talk to about those good old days."

"Oh, who?" But before Ginny could answer, a maid came out of the house and over to them. "The florist is here, Miss Ryan. He wants to know if he can have a word with you about the flowers for the living room."

"Oh, yes, I'll be right there," Caitlin replied. She turned to excuse herself to Ginny, but her friend had heard and was already backing away. With a nod to Caitlin, Ginny headed across the lawn toward the pool.

Reaching the pool area, Ginny paused, trying to decide whether to stop and say hello to Laurence and Melanie. But they both seemed so engrossed in their conversation that she kept on going. She headed toward a striped tent that had been set up on the lawn not far from the pool. Inside, the caterers were serving lunch. She suddenly realized how hungry she was.

Melanie saw Ginny looking in her direction and crossed her fingers, hoping that Caitlin's friend would not come over. She breathed a sigh of relief as Ginny moved on. At that moment Melanie wanted to be alone with Laurence. *Too bad we're not on a deserted tropical island*, she thought.

*Life is strange*, she mused. It had been over a year since she had even given Laurence Baxter so much as a passing thought. Now, here he was, and her heart was beating wildly in her chest. She felt as if a shock were going through her when they had bumped into each other a few hours earlier. The electricity she had felt ran in a straight line up her arm from where he touched her. She still felt tingly.

She was fairly certain that Laurence felt something, too. It was as if they had both become mesmerized. After helping themselves to lunch, they had sat down on the chaises to eat. But neither of them had touched the food. Once they started talking, they couldn't seem to stop. Laurence immediately wanted to know what she had been up to in the past couple of years. And she wanted to tell him.

"I've been so busy this term that I really haven't had a chance to do much except study," she said. She crossed one slim, tanned leg over the other, and she leaned forward, her elbow on her knee.

"So you're just going to bum around this summer, huh?"

"Ummm—yes. I was thinking of going to Italy for a month, maybe even Greece." Her clear green eyes sparkled as she added, "Well, maybe not that far."

Laurence laughed, and his handsome features softened. "Virginia's a great place in the summertime."

"Yes, so I've heard," she replied cautiously.

"So, is there anyone special in your life right now?" Laurence's tone was lightly teasing.

She shrugged nonchalantly, but her heart was pounding. "No—no one." She looked over at him. "What about you?"

"Me? Oh, I've been throwing myself into my work at the Madison *Intelligencer*," he said, acting as though he had misunderstood her question. "I know it's only a small paper, but it's a good one. And I've even got a by-line."

"What ever happened to your work in Washington? I know you moved there."

"Yes, but just for a while. I guess I'm just a small town boy at heart," Laurence admitted. "I didn't like the dirt and the crowds, and I changed my mind. I guess I prefer living where the air is clean and the people are friendly."

She nodded, understanding. "Sometimes I feel that way about New York. It has to be the most exciting place in the world to live, but sometimes I'll be walking down the street and the crowds and noise will really get to me. Then I think about how nice it would be to be back in Montana walking beside a mountain stream. Or riding a horse across an open plain. You can ride for miles out there and never see another person."

"You know, I can imagine you doing just that," Laurence said. "It's strange that we never went riding together. Maybe we could sometime this weekend." His warm brown eyes were inviting. "There are a lot of beautiful trails on the estate, and you'd have your pick of horses."

"That sounds like fun," Melanie answered, trying to keep her voice even. The whole time, though, she could feel her blood racing because of the way he was looking at her. She wanted to reach out and run her fingers through his wavy hair.

Finally she turned away. She glanced around, desperately searching for something noncommittal to say. Thankfully, two people emerging from the house just then caught Melanie's eye.

"Oh!" Melanie smiled. "There's Jed—and

Caitlin. He's here." She glanced back at Laurence. "Let's go up and say hi."

"Yeah, sure," Laurence said with a smile. "I'd really like to say hi to Jed." Getting lazily to his feet, he reached for her hand to help her up. As she took it, the warmth of his hand sent another charge through her. "Then afterward," he said, "maybe we can talk to Caitlin about those horses."

## 2

Caitlin fastened her emerald and diamond necklace around her slender throat, then stepped back from the antique mirror that stood in a corner of her bedroom. She studied her reflection. The dress she was wearing had been designed especially for her by Jerome of Georgetown. Made of royal blue taffeta, it had a finely pleated, strapless bodice that gave way to a full, swirling skirt. There was also a huge, crisp bow in the back. Caitlin had never looked more beautiful.

Lifting her hand to her hair, she feathered a ringlet. As she did, the sparkle of her engagement ring caught her eye. With a smile, she looked down at her hand and decided that she couldn't possibly be any happier than she was at that moment. She had looked forward to getting engaged to Jed for what seemed like forever. Quickly she made a vow to herself that she would allow nothing, absolutely nothing, to ruin that happiness.

With that in mind, she went downstairs to check on everything one last time.

Her first stop was the kitchen, where she found that Mrs. Crowley, the family cook, had everything well in hand. She was briskly barking orders at the extra help that had been hired for the evening. The whole room smelled delicious, and Caitlin saw that the hors d'oeuvres were already being arranged on the platters.

Reassured, she went into the living room. All the furniture in the room had been pushed against the walls to allow room for dancing. And at one end of the long room, an area had been reserved for the five-piece orchestra. They had just arrived and were beginning to set up. They would play during dinner, as well as for the dancing later. Walking the length of the room, she noticed that the flowers that had been arranged on the side tables looked perfect. Before leaving, she stopped long enough to check that the orchestra leader had her list of musical selections.

From the living room, she went into the dining room. Margaret, the maid, was there, checking the table settings. With care, she moved a spoon a fraction of an inch to one side. As Caitlin entered the room, the older woman stood tall and smiled. "Just checking to see that everything looks all right, Miss Caitlin."

"The room looks lovely, doesn't it?" Caitlin replied. The gold-rimmed Ainsley china had been set out along with the heavy antique silver flatwear and delicate Waterford crystal. Slender white candles were placed in silver candlesticks, ready to be lit just before the guests were seated. A low centerpiece of yellow- and salmon-colored roses had been placed on each of the tables that had been set up to accommodate the large group. "Did you double check the place cards against the table diagrams I drew up?"

"Yes, miss," Margaret replied with a nod. "And Mrs. Crowley has assured me that dinner will be perfect."

"I'm sure it will be," Caitlin said with a smile, not telling her that she had just checked. "I guess I'll just go and wait for my guests to start arriving." As she turned, she gave a little start as she saw her grandmother standing in the doorway, watching her.

Caitlin noticed the look in Regina Ryan's sharp blue eyes—she was judging Caitlin's performance as a hostess. In the past her grandmother would have handled all the details for the party. But she was getting older, and she no longer had the strength to do it all. "Grandmother," Caitlin said, smiling slightly nervously. "I didn't hear you."

Mrs. Ryan returned the smile. Although illness had aged her, she still retained her regal bearing. In addition to her bearing, steel blue eyes and high-cheekboned features gave her the kind of beauty that age could not diminish. Her silver hair was swept back from her face in a simple, but elegant style, and she was dressed in a floor-length shift of deep blue silk, shot through with silver.

"You've done a lovely job, Caitlin. I wanted to tell you that before the others came down."

"Why thank you, Grandmother," Caitlin said happily.

"I think we still have time for a glass of sherry in the library. Will you join me?"

"Of course," Caitlin agreed, giving her grandmother a questioning look. The suggestion had set off a warning bell inside Caitlin's head. Years of living under Regina Ryan's domineering thumb made Caitlin wonder if there was something on her grandmother's mind—something she wanted from Caitlin.

But Mrs. Ryan either didn't see Caitlin's questioning look, or purposefully ignored it. Putting a slender, wrinkled hand on Caitlin's arm, she steered her out of the dining room.

"You've been so busy this weekend, and we haven't really had much of a chance to chat. And you know," she went on amiably, "I always find that if I can manage to steal a few minutes for myself before a party I'm a much more relaxed hostess."

Caitlin nodded politely, still wondering what could be going on.

"And the glass of sherry never hurt, either," Mrs. Ryan added, with a rare show of gentle humor.

Entering the library, Caitlin helped her grandmother to sit down on the couch. The richly polished wood and shelves of old books, many bound in softly faded leather, gleamed in the soft light. Potted plants had been massed in the marble fireplace, and a formal arrangement of flowers from the conservatory sat on a Regency table. Caitlin crossed to the sideboard, where she poured the golden-colored liquid into two glasses. Handing one to her grandmother, she sat down opposite her in a wing back chair. Sipping at the sweet heavy wine, she watched her grandmother take a single sip, then set her glass down on the low mahogany coffee table between them. With a delicate sigh, she rested her hands in her lap and said, "It's fortunate the weather's been so lovely. Not even a hint of rain."

"Yes," Caitlin replied, nodding. She tried to relax, but the warning bell was still ringing inside her head. "It has been lovely. Jed and I are thinking about getting up early tomorrow and going for a long ride before the others get up."

"That's a wonderful idea," her grandmother agreed. "In fact, Jed and I had a nice little talk about the horses this afternoon." Picking up her glass, she took a sip, then put it down again. "Poor Duster," she said, shaking her head. Duster was the Thoroughbred gelding Caitlin had raised from a yearling and trained herself.

"Why, what's wrong with him?" Caitlin asked, a frown creasing her forehead. "I just went down to visit him before I went up to get dressed. He was fine."

"That's just the problem," Mrs. Ryan nodded. "He is healthy, and he isn't being ridden. That horse is one of the best hunters in the area. He should be worked all summer, then hunted in the fall. It's such a waste for him to be cooped up in that stall all the time." She bent to pick up her glass. "I no longer ride or I'd exercise him myself."

It was not exactly an accusation, but Caitlin felt a stab of guilt at her grandmother's words. It really was a shame that all the hard work she had put into training Duster was now being wasted. It would probably be better to just sell him to someone who could ride him more often, but she just couldn't bear to part with him. Still, it wasn't fair to keep him as a kind of long-distance pet. "Maybe I could make a point of coming down here a couple of weekends a month," she suggested. But even as she said it, she knew that the suggestion was impractical.

"Hmmm—perhaps." Mrs. Ryan shrugged delicately. She sat back again. "You know, you would have more time to ride him if you started taking an interest in Ryan Mining. You would be here—"

"Now, Grandmother!" Caitlin cried. So this was what the warning bell was forecasting. Even since Caitlin had been in high school, Regina Ryan had been trying to talk her granddaughter into taking over as president of Ryan Mining when she was ready to retire. But Caitlin had just as firmly resisted, wanting to decide her career plans for herself.

"Caitlin, I only want what's best for you— and for Ryan Mining. You and the company are the most important things in my life."

"Oh, Grandmother!" Caitlin sighed, her voice sounding exasperated but kind. "Why won't you listen to me? My life is just the way I want it. I have a great job, and so does Jed. He's with a very prestigious law firm, and I'm sure that one day he'll be asked to become a partner. I couldn't begin to run Ryan Mining from New York, even if I wanted to. And I don't."

"Jed could find a job with a law firm down here," Mrs. Ryan insisted. "A law firm is a law firm. But a family company is—well, just that, a *family* company. And I want it to stay that way."

"Grandmother, please!" Caitlin was becoming a bit agitated. "Now is not the time to go into this. If I had known you wanted to talk about Ryan Mining, I wouldn't have come in here with you." She rose, putting her glass down on the table with such force that it almost shattered.

"Caitlin—" Mrs. Ryan's eyebrows arched slightly as she gave Caitlin an admonishing look. Caitlin remembered the look vividly from her childhood, and it always made her feel about ten years old again.

"Sorry, Grandmother," she said, apologizing automatically.

"That's all right. I forgive you," Mrs. Ryan said with a hint of righteousness in her voice. "I know you're just thinking about your guests. But I also feel it important that we discuss this. I have so little time left, and I can't help but worry about matters that I consider important. They must be taken care of before I'm gone."

"Grandmother, don't be ridiculous," Caitlin protested. She forced a smile, hoping her grandmother wouldn't notice the falseness of it. "You're not going to die for a long time. The doctor even said—"

"Those doctors know nothing!" Mrs. Ryan snapped with such energy that Caitlin wondered if her grandmother had been exaggerating her illness just a bit. And, then, just thinking that made Caitlin feel guilty and ashamed. *Damn it,* she thought. When was she going to stop letting her grandmother manipulate her?

In an even voice Caitlin said, "I'm sorry, but I really must go see to my guests. I can hear them." But even as she spoke, she found herself weakening. She added, "We can talk more about this later, okay?" As she walked toward the door, though, she told herself firmly that she would do everything in her power to avoid discussing the subject again.

Dinner for Caitlin and her house guests was sumptuous. It began with cold, poached salmon, followed by a lemon sorbet. Then came Cornish game hens stuffed with a mixture of wild rice, walnuts, and currants, accompanied by asparagus. The salad was served after the main entree. Dessert was a chocolate mousse so rich no one could eat more than a few bites.

Fresh brewed coffee was served with it, and everyone lingered in the dining room for a while before Caitlin suggested they go into the living room for dancing.

Entering the room on Jed's arm, she nodded to the orchestra leader, and he struck up the melody she had requested he play to start the dancing. It was a song that she and Jed had danced to years before, when they had first started going together. As the sweet opening notes floated across the room, she looked up into Jed's eyes. "Remember this?" she asked softly.

Jed's answer was a loving smile as he took her in his arms and swept her around the room. Their friends soon joined them also whirling across the polished floor.

Not long after that, the guests who had been invited to come after dinner began to arrive. Soon the huge room was crowded with laughing, happy young couples.

As the hostess, Caitlin made sure to say hello to each of her guests, chatting with each between dances. When she finally got a chance to relax for a moment, she went to get a glass of punch.

Crossing the room, however, she couldn't help but notice how wrapped up in each other Melanie and Laurence seemed to be, almost to the exlusion of anyone else in the room. It worried her. The way Melanie was acting made her wonder if Laurence had told her that he already had a girlfriend. Caitlin made up her mind to have a few words with Jed's sister.

Her chance came while the orchestra took a break. Melanie was alone, standing near one of the open french doors. Excusing herself from the group she and Jed were talking to, she walked over to Melanie and suggested they go out onto the terrace.

"Melanie," Caitlin said seriously, touching the younger girl's arm lightly, "please don't think I'm meddling, but I couldn't help noticing how well you and Laurence have been getting along tonight."

"Oh, is that all?" Melanie let out a relieved laugh. "For a minute I thought something terrible had happened." Even in the semidarkness of the stone terrace, Melanie's eyes sparkled with happiness. She giggled and spun around dreamily.

"Oh, Caitlin, I can't believe the way I feel about him. It's almost like love at first sight—except that we did go out a few times. But he's so different now, more exciting—more mature." She looked at Caitlin eagerly. "Is it my imagination, or is he really more handsome now?"

"Melanie"— Caitlin's hand tightened on her arm— "Melanie, has Laurence told you about Nancy?"

"Nancy?"

"His girlfriend. Melanie, he's dating some-one—seriously. She's not at the party tonight because she has the flu." Caitlin paused, waiting for a reaction, but there was none. "Melanie?"

"That can't be, Caitlin."

"I'm sorry, but it's true."

"No. No way," Melanie said, denying it. She pulled away from Caitlin. "Maybe he was dating someone before this weekend," she said in a firm tone. "But not anymore. We've even made plans for tomorrow."

"Plans?" Caitlin asked. "What kind of plans?"

"Oh, you know, a drive in the country, dinner at a little inn." She shrugged happily. "Just a romantic little getaway. Laurence told me he wanted to go someplace where we could be completely alone."

"Why?" Caitlin felt a sudden tightening in her stomach.

"What do you mean, why?" Melanie shot Caitlin a questioning look.

"Well, it sounds more like you're running away from someone—or somebody—than simply planning a nice day together."

"Oh, Caitlin, honestly!" Melanie cried, rolling her eyes. "Just because Laurence wants to make sure we're going to have some privacy doesn't mean we're running away from anyone." She shook her head. "Caitlin, please don't do this."

"I'm sorry, Melanie, but I just can't ignore the fact that Laurence isn't being honest with you. This date sounds very secretive—like something he wants to keep Nancy from hearing about."

"You're so wrong about him," Melanie insisted.

"I really hope I am," Caitlin said unhappily. "Do me a favor, ask him about Nancy."

"No, I won't." Melanie shook her head emphatically. "I might as well come right out and accuse him of having a girlfriend he's not telling me about." Unreasonably, she added, "Besides, it doesn't matter if he does. Nothing that happened before this weekend matters."

"But, Melanie—"

Caitlin stopped abruptly when the very person they'd been discussing came out onto the terrace.

"There you are," Laurence called. An uneasy look passed over his face as he recognized Caitlin, but then he went on smoothly, "I leave you for two seconds to go ask the orchestra to play a song for you, and you take off." He looked directly at Caitlin, his eyes daring her to expose him. "And what's so interesting that it dragged you two from one of the best parties I've been to in ages?" he asked lightly.

"Thank you for the compliment, Laurence," Caitlin said graciously, if a bit stiffly. "And it was only girl talk. I'm sure you wouldn't be interested. But maybe Melanie will fill you in later," she added pointedly, casting a meaningful glance in Melanie's direction.

But Melanie ignored it. "Caitlin's right," she told Laurence sweetly. "It would bore you." Nodding in the direction of the living room, she asked, "Is this the song you asked them to play?" He nodded and she smiled as the lovely melody drifted out onto the terrace. "Oh, Laurence, I love this song. How did you know?"

"You mentioned it this afternoon," he replied easily. He tightened his arm around Melanie's waist. "Now, come on, let's go in there and dance to it before it's over." He glanced at Caitlin. "You'll excuse us, won't you, Caitlin?" he asked, leading Melanie away before Caitlin could answer.

As she watched the two step back inside the house, she sighed. No matter what Melanie said, the meeting they had planned for the next day did sound secretive. And a secret meeting with someone else's boyfriend couldn't possibly end happily.

The party was over. The orchestra had packed up and gone home. The extra staff that had been hired for the party had also left, and the servants had all retired. The house guests were in their rooms, and the last of the party stragglers had finally driven away in their Porsches and BMWs.

Jed and Caitlin were standing on the terrace saying a private good night. Caitlin had already decided she wouldn't ruin the evening by mentioning Melanie and Laurence. Besides, maybe Melanie would come to her senses and confront Laurence about Nancy before she went off with him.

Caitlin did, however, mention the conversation she had had with her grandmother before dinner. "Jed, I just can't help it. Every time she brings up Ryan Mining lately, I feel guilty. I know how much she wants me to say I'll take over as president, but I just can't. It isn't for me. But every time I try to explain that to her she refuses to *really* listen."

"I know," Jed said and slipped his arms around her waist, pulling her to him and resting his chin on the top of her head. "Your grandmother's a stubborn woman. And that company is so terribly important to her—more important than you sometimes. I don't doubt that she would stoop to almost anything to get you involved in Ryan Mining."

"You're right," Caitlin said with a little sigh. She pulled away from him and looked up into his eyes.

"You'd better believe I am. You were right to stick to your guns. You hang in there, she'll come around. Sooner or later, she'll understand that our future is in New York, and there's no room for Ryan Mining in our lives."

"That's exactly what I told her."

"So, just don't let her change your mind," he whispered gently. "And don't feel guilty for living your life the way you want to. If you want to be a writer then be a writer." He looked into her eyes and saw only uncertainty there. "If you let her bully you, you'll just be miserable."

"Don't worry. I won't," Caitlin promised, her tone earnest. She smiled and raised her hand to run her fingers through his thick hair. Then she let her hand slide down so she could trace a line lightly along the length of his jaw. "My life is with you, and only you," she said softly.

"And don't you ever forget it," he warned softly as he pulled her closer to him.

"Oh, Jed, I love you so very much."

"Not more than I love you," he replied. Then his mouth gently covered hers. She was breathless when they finally parted. With a happy sigh, she leaned her head against his shoulder. They stood there together, simply enjoying being with each other in the sweet, dark summer night.

## 3

The day was bright and cloudless when Melanie pulled her rental car into the parking area in front of the Chef's Inn, where she had agreed to meet Laurence. Hers was the only car in the wide, asphalt lot. Glancing at her watch, she saw it was ten-forty. Laurence was ten minutes late. She frowned at herself. She was late, too. What if he was on time, saw that she wasn't there, and decided she wasn't coming? He could have already been there and left. She bit her lip. She really shouldn't have stopped at that coffee shop. But she'd been twenty minutes early, and she hadn't wanted him to think she was too eager.

*No, he'll be here*, she reassured herself. It was only ten minutes. Maybe traffic had been bad, or he had had some kind of car trouble. Yes, it had to be something that simple.

She leaned back against the seat. Then, too nervous to sit still, she dug into her purse for her compact. Flipping it open, she looked into the little mirror to check her makeup. She was only wearing eyeliner and a little mascara, much less than she normally wore in New York. She remembered that Laurence had mentioned he preferred the clean, outdoorsy type. With that in mind, she had put on a simple, sleeveless dress of chocolate brown linen, which set off her tan. On her feet were sandals of light tan leather to match the belt that circled her narrow waist. She ran her fingers through her mop of brown curls, fluffing them out. Then she put the compact back in her purse.

She checked her watch again. Five minutes had passed. Her heart jumped a little in her chest. What if Laurence had had second thoughts and decided not to come after all? It was possible. Plans made at night sometimes didn't seem the same the next morning. Without wanting to, she started thinking about what Caitlin had said to her. Did Laurence really have a girlfriend named Nancy? And, if he did, why hadn't he mentioned her? She felt a sudden sting behind her eyes and her throat tightened. Was Laurence just toying with her—just having fun because his date couldn't make it to the party? No—no, it couldn't be anything like that. She closed her eyes and took a deep breath. She remembered the way Laurence had looked at her the day before, his warm eyes sparkling. *That was no act*, she assured herself. Opening her eyes, she saw Laurence standing beside the car. He was looking down at her, smiling.

"Oh!" she said, both startled and happy. "I didn't hear you drive up."

"You must have been lost in thought. I hope you were thinking about me," he said teasingly.

"I was," she admitted. Then she blushed at her own forwardness.

"Fantastic!" He chuckled. "I couldn't ask for more." Opening the car door he helped her out. "You look great."

"Oh, thank you." She looked at him, and though she didn't say it, she thought he looked even handsomer than he had the day before—if that were possible. He was dressed casually, in a dark green polo shirt, and wheat-colored slacks.

After she locked her car, he led her to his car. It was a black, Mustang convertible, and the top was down. "I hope you don't mind," he said, motioning to the top.

"No, I love it," she said, laughing. "I love the wind in my hair."

"Good." He smiled and added, "I had a feeling you would."

He pulled out of the parking lot and turned onto the road that led out of town. "I hope you like what I've planned for the day."

"I'm sure I will," she murmured and smiled back at him. The way she felt at that moment, he could have suggested walking on hot coals and she would have thought that sounded marvelous.

Melanie took a sip of coffee, smiling as she remembered the previous day—and night. After having lunch at a charming out-of-the-way inn, they got back into the car and Laurence drove Melanie all around the country-side. They even bought kites and tried to fly them in a field, but it wasn't windy enough. Finally they headed back to Laurence's apartment to cook dinner. Melanie insisted on buying ice cream, but they never got to it.

It was still sitting unopened in the freezer compartment of Laurence's refrigerator the next morning at breakfast. Melanie had already made coffee and squeezed some oranges for fresh juice. There was also toast. She had wanted to make eggs, too, but there weren't any. Still, they could share what she had made. She could hear the shower being turned off and knew he would be out shortly. *This*, she thought with a shy smile, *is what it would be like if we lived together.*

And there was no reason why they couldn't, at least, live closer to each other. She had been thinking about it ever since she woke up. She decided to talk to him about her idea as soon as he had had his first cup of coffee.

Keyed up, she rose and went over to the counter. She poured some coffee into a cup as Laurence came into the room and handed it to him.

"Good morning," he said, leaning down to kiss her as he accepted the cup from her. "Ah, smells good."

"Good morning back," she said with a smile. Looking up at him, his hair still wet from the shower, his skin smelling of good soap, she decided he was more handsome than ever.

"Laurence, I've had the most wonderful idea—" She paused just long enough so she knew she had his attention. "This weekend has been so terrific, and, well—I don't want it to end."

"I'll second that," he agreed easily, sitting. "And we're definitely going to have to do it again."

41

"Well—" Melanie shrugged nervously. It wasn't going to be quite so easy as she had hoped it would be. "What I meant was, I don't want it to end. And it doesn't have to."

"I don't understand."

"I've been thinking—I've already decided to take time off from school before going back to graduate school" —she shrugged— "I really don't know how much time at this point, but what I'm thinking is—I could move down here, to Virginia."

"Here?"

"Yes, silly," she said and laughed lightly. Why, she wondered, was he being so dense. "I want to be with you, all the time. Well, as much of the time as possible, anyway," she added as she joined him at the table. "I was thinking that with my degree in communications, I could get a job at one of the TV stations near here. Maybe I could even apply for some kind of job on the paper you work for— assistant editor or something. That's the kind of job they give people right out of college, isn't it?"

"Melanie . . ." Laurence began, looking uncomfortable. "Uh—I don't know quite what to say."

"Say you think it's a great idea," she replied.

He looked at her for a long moment, then shook his head. "To be perfectly honest, I hadn't expected anything like this."

"What do you mean? You do like me, don't you?" She looked at him, noticing his uneasy expression for the first time.

"Well, sure, I mean, we've had a great time, but—" He put his hand lightly on her arm.

"But, that's all." She stared at him, nodding slowly. She shook her head, mumbling, "Oh, boy, Melanie, are you ever dumb."

"Melanie, please! Let me explain."

"You don't have to, I understand completely. As far as you're concerned, this was just a one-night stand." Taking a deep breath, she let it out slowly and set her cup down. "I get it now. You were free for the weekend because your girlfriend has the flu, or something, so you decided not to waste it. When you saw me, you figured it would be great fun to spend the night with dear old Melanie. Right?"

"No! No, of course not," Laurence protested. "I really care about you, it's just that— Look, we've had a great time together, but now you instantly want to turn it into some kind of major relationship." He rubbed his forehead. "It's all so sudden."

"That should be my line," Melanie retorted. She looked at him for a moment, then shook her head slowly. "It's true, isn't it? About this Nancy person? Caitlin tried to warn me, but I wouldn't listen. I couldn't believe that you could care for someone else after the way things were between us yesterday"—her voice dropped nearly to a whisper—"and last night."

Laurence didn't answer right away. Instead he stood up and went over to the counter to refill his coffee cup. When he turned back toward her, he didn't answer her question directly. "I'm just not ready for the kind of relationship you're talking about." He leaned back against the counter. "And, to be perfectly honest, yes, I still do have feelings for Nancy Robinson. We've been going together for quite a while. Those kind of feelings don't go away."

"Don't you think you should have told me about her before I let myself get involved with you?"

"I was going to—several times," Laurence said slowly. "But I chickened out." He shrugged. "I guess I just didn't want to spoil everything. I mean, you looked so happy, and I—"

"Oh, great!" Melanie could feel the tears building in her eyes, but she was determined not to cry. "It would have been pretty dumb on your part to tell me. Just keep gullible Melanie going, right? Because you knew just how fast I would have walked away if I'd known I was just a weekend fling."

"Oh, come on, Melanie," Laurence protested. "It wasn't like that at all." He started toward her.

She stood up, backing a step away from him toward the living room area. Her voice was low and slightly shaky. "You are a slime, Laurence Baxter—a total slime." But a second after she had said the words, she regretted them. She spoke again, this time calmly and quietly. "Oh, well, I suppose I should at least thank you for being honest with me this morning. At least you didn't let me continue thinking you meant all those things you said last night. Well, uh—goodbye, Laurence."

Walking quickly over to the couch, she picked up her purse and crossed over to the apartment door. Melanie forced herself to keep from slamming it shut behind her. Only after she was out in the hall did she let the tears roll down her cheeks and wonder how she was going to get to her car at the Chef's Inn.

Caitlin sipped her third cup of coffee. She was sitting at the white wrought iron table on the terrace. Margaret had just cleared away her breakfast dishes. Caitlin had barely touched the poached eggs and fresh blueberry muffin Mrs. Crowley had fixed for her.

She couldn't eat because she was so worried

about Melanie. The last she had heard from Jed's sister was the note she left the morning before saying she was going to be spending the day with Laurence. Caitlin was relatively certain Melanie hadn't been hurt. If she had been, Caitlin reasoned, she would have heard. But an accident wasn't the worst thing that could happen to someone. A broken heart could hurt just as much. She shook her head. If only Melanie would call.

Setting down her cup, Caitlin lifted the top off the sugar bowl, picked up a cube with the silver tongs, and added it to her coffee. She stirred it absently. At least Jed had gone back to New York the night before so he didn't know that his sister had spent the night out. Lucky, too, that the last of the house guests had left only an hour before so there wouldn't be anyone wondering where Melanie was—or where she had been all night.

*Now, if only I knew*, Caitlin thought.

Just then she heard the sound of quiet footsteps crossing the stone terrace. Glancing up, she saw Melanie coming in the door. Relief and compassion flooded through Caitlin as she saw Melanie's swollen eyes and tear-streaked face.

She ran over to Jed's sister. "Melanie—oh, Melanie, honey." She held out her arms and enfolded Melanie in them. The younger girl's tears began all over again.

# 4

Later that afternoon Caitlin and Melanie were on their way back to New York. Melanie, sitting in the window seat, had not said a word since they had boarded the plane at Dulles Airport. She kept her head turned toward the window and stared morosely out at the banks of clouds.

Looking over at Melanie, Caitlin felt a rush of sympathy. Laurence's behavior really had been shabby. But then, Caitlin thought, it was probably best that the relationship had ended as quickly as it had. Melanie could have been hurt much worse. Still, Caitlin couldn't help remembering Melanie's unhappy words as they sat together in the living room at Ryan Acres.

"Oh, Caitlin," she had said. "In spite of

everything, I still care about him. I can't bear the thought of having to live without him."

Caitlin hoped the distance separating them would help Melanie get over those feelings. She picked up the fashion magazine that lay in her lap and began flipping idly through the pages. She was going to see to it that Melanie had something to distract her from her thoughts of Laurence Baxter. Perhaps an interesting, part-time job would help. Or maybe a trip. France was beautiful in the summer—much better than hot, sticky New York.

She put the magazine down. In spite of the hot weather, thinking about the city made her smile. Jed was there. In only a few hours he would be coming over to her apartment for dinner. And, much as she cared about Melanie's problems, she was going to put them aside, at least for the night—this night was for her and Jed only.

Caitlin quickly settled back into the routine of her job as a writer with *National News*. Immediately she was caught up in several interesting stories. She flew up to Vermont to interview a man who made hand-blown glassware, then to eastern Canada to talk to a wildlife filmmaker. Back in New York she interviewed a wealthy socialite who was accused of stealing from her friends.

Still, she managed to find time to have lunch with Melanie quite often. One afternoon they decided to browse through some of the art galleries in SoHo. As far as Caitlin could tell, Melanie was bouncing back from her brief fling with Laurence. As they stood together looking at a brightly colored oil painting, Caitlin casually asked if she had been seeing anyone in particular lately.

At first, she wasn't certain Melanie had heard her because she just continued to stare at the painting. But at last she looked over at Caitlin. "If you're asking if I'm over Laurence, I'm not sure. I'm trying . . ." she said and shook her head sadly. "It's going to take time, though."

"I know," Caitlin replied, nodding sympathetically. "And I didn't mean to pry. It's just that I'd hate to see him hurt you. I really think that—"

"Laurence was just using me," Melanie said, finishing Caitlin's sentence. "Something like that, right? I agree with you. What he pulled was unforgivable. But it's just not that simple." She shrugged helplessly. "I wish it were."

Seeing how upset her friend was getting, Caitlin quickly put her hand on Melanie's arm and gave her a comforting smile. "You know what I think, I've had enough of these paintings. What do you say to getting some iced tea somewhere. Or," she added, her eyes twinkling, "maybe we should indulge ourselves and get some ice cream instead."

"With chocolate sauce, nuts, and lots of whipped cream," Melanie agreed with a laugh.

"Absolutely!" And Caitlin laughed back.


At the end of July the city was hit by the first major heat wave of the summer. The temperature soared into the nineties.

"I'd give my right arm to be lying beside the pool or on the beach at some secluded island hotel," Caitlin said, listlessly poking at her salad with her fork. She looked up at Jed. "I'm so sick of this humidity, I could die. If only I could smell some fresh air for a change."

"Great minds work alike," Jed said, smiling. "And it just so happens that Jim, one of the associates at the office, invited us to go surfing at Montauk this weekend. It's not exactly Hawaii, but it would be fun just to get my feet on a surfboard again. What do you think?"

A frown creased Caitlin's face. "Oh, Jed, I'd love to go to the beach, but I don't like the idea of you surfing. It's so dangerous. Couldn't we make it some other time?"

Jed continued to smile. "What would I do without you to look out for me, Caitlin?" he asked, tousling her hair. "All right, I'll tell Jim we can't make it. But what do you say to a weekend on Cape Cod? The beach, swimming in the bay, fresh fish for dinner—and absolutely no surfing."

"Maybe even a clambake," Caitlin suggested. "And afterward, we could walk across the sand in the moonlight." She grinned. "Fabulous, when do we leave?"

"How about this weekend? I could make reservations and we could fly up on Friday night. In time for that fish dinner."

"Oh, Jed, let's," Caitlin said, a smile lighting up her face.

On Thursday night Caitlin was standing in front of her closet trying to decide what to pack for the weekend when the phone rang. Thinking it must be Jed, she picked it up and gaily said, "Hello!"

A moment later she sat down on the edge of the bed, her knees had suddenly collapsed under her. "I'm so sorry to have to tell you like this, honey," her father said. "I thought about coming up there so I could tell you in person, but then I decided you would rather know immediately so you could make plans to fly down here."

"Yes, yes, of course," Caitlin answered in stunned tones. "When did it happen?"

"This afternoon. Rollins said she went upstairs to take a nap and left word with Margaret to wake her at four. When Margaret went up later, she was gone." Dr. Westlake's voice was gentle. "Caitlin, she probably never even knew what was happening. It was the best way."

"Yes, we should be thankful for that, at least." She closed her eyes for a second to think. "I'll leave right away. I'll have to leave word at work, of course—and I'll have to tell Jed," she said, tears beginning to choke her voice.

After hanging up, she sat as if paralyzed, her hand still on the phone, tears streaming down her cheeks.

*Grandmother's dead.*

It wasn't true. It couldn't be, her mind kept insisting. She had always thought her grandmother would live forever. Caitlin couldn't imagine Ryan Acres—or her life—without her grandmother.

Maybe there was a mistake, Caitlin thought irrationally.

But no, her father definitely said her grandmother had died in her sleep. A second and fatal stroke.

She had to call Jed. Lifting the receiver to her ear, Caitlin began dialing.

Jed provided a solid shoulder for Caitlin. After seeing her off at the airport, he promised to fly down the following evening. He'd be there for the funeral, which Caitlin had already decided would be either on Monday or Tuesday. But he was still concerned about her and didn't want to leave her alone. When he told Melanie she offered to go to Virginia with Caitlin.

For Caitlin, the next three days moved in a slow, wrenching blur. At times she felt more like a robot than a person—taking care of everything but not feeling anything. There were so many things to be done, arrangements to be made.

She had to choose the time and place for the service, decide on the right casket, and pick out the music that would be played. Of course, her father and Jed helped her as much as they could. Her father suggested she arrange for a private service.

"Your grandmother was a very well-known woman, and I think you'll get a lot of curious onlookers if you don't," he said as they were walking down the steps of the funeral home on Saturday.

"Yes, I guess you're probably right," Caitlin agreed. Glancing up at Jed, who was walking on her other side, she went on, "I'm so afraid it's going to turn into a terrible circus, no matter what we do." A frown gently creased her brow. "And there's the press, too."

"Don't worry," Jed replied, slipping a protective arm around her shoulders. "I won't let any of them get near you."

She leaned her head briefly against his comforting chest. "Thank you," she said softly. Then she looked back at her father, so strong and handsome. "Thank you, too. I don't know how I would have gotten through all of this if it weren't for you and Jed."

"You would have, honey," he replied, taking her hand and squeezing it gently. "You're a lot stronger than you think you are. But I'll always be here for you—I promise."


In those first days before the funeral there was an almost constant stream of visitors to Ryan Acres. Most stayed only long enough to pay their respects or remember Regina in some kind way. On Sunday afternoon, however, Rollins came to the door of the library where Caitlin was going through some of her grandmother's private correspondence. Standing just beside him was Randolph Woods, the current lawyer for Ryan Mining. With him were two older men she recognized only vaguely as members of the board. A sinking feeling formed in the pit of her stomach as she rose from the desk and went over to them, her hand outstretched. "Mr. Woods, gentlemen—hello." She shook hands with each of them, then motioned toward some chairs. "Won't you sit down."

There was a moment of silence as the men sat down. Then the two older men looked at Mr. Woods and nodded.

Randolph Woods cleared his throat. "I'm really terribly sorry to bother you at this time, so soon after Mrs. Ryan's death, but I'm afraid I must." He cleared his throat again. "As heir to your grandmother's interest in Ryan Mining, you must understand the need for us to discuss with you who will be taking over as head of the company." He glanced at the other two, as if for moral support.

"Yes, indeed, it's most important," the heavier gentleman said. His name was Mr. Gottlieb, she thought. "What is important is that company matters move smoothly right now—that there's an easy transition of power."

"Indeed, indeed," the other man added

quickly. "We don't want to let anything fall through the cracks, as it might during a long executive search."

"I see." Caitlin looked thoughtful for a moment. "Well, how can I help you?"

The three men exchanged glances. Mr. Woods looked Caitlin directly in the eyes. "We would like you to take over as president of Ryan Mining," he said.

"You what?" Her stomach felt as if someone had just punched it—hard. She ran a hand through her hair. "I'm flattered, but I'll—um, I'll need time to think about it."

That evening she told Jed about the meeting. It was after dinner and they were walking in the garden, the soft summer twilight descending around them.

"Oh, Jed, it was like they'd tossed me a five hundred-pound rock and told me not to drop it," she said, stopping to look up at him.

"It must have been a terrible shock," he said. "And I think it was rotten of them to come talk to you about business at a time like this—on a Sunday, no less."

"I know," she agreed. "But I do understand their point. After all, they have to think of Ryan Mining. My grandmother's death wasn't a personal loss for them, it was a business loss."

"So, what did you tell them?" Jed asked. He took her hands. "I hope you said no."

"Actually, I didn't give them a definite answer." She met Jed's green eyes with her blue ones. "I told them I would give them my decision at the office on Tuesday morning."

"Which means," he replied in a worried tone, "that you're actually considering their proposal?"

"It means that I wanted time to think about it, about what would be best for everyone." She pulled free from his grasp and turned away. "I'm going to tell them I will do whatever is required for the company," she said in a whisper.

"What?" Jed stared at her incredulously. "Why? Is it guilt? Surely running Ryan Mining isn't what you really want, is it? I mean, all those years you resisted your grandmother." He shook his head. "Why are you giving in now? I don't understand."

"I guess at first I didn't understand myself," she said, then smiled up at him. "I'm not feeling guilty, Jed. It's just that—I'm a Ryan. That company has my family's name on it. I'm not going to let my grandmother down—I can't."

Jed nodded silently. He could understand

her feelings, even though he didn't approve of what she had decided. "Would you like me to stay and be with you at the meeting?" He slipped his hands gently around her waist.

"Oh, that's sweet of you," she said with a smile. "And I'd love to have you stay. But you already took Friday off and you'll be here for me tomorrow. You'd better go back. Besides, I'd really rather stand on my own at the meeting. Anyway, what I'm going to say isn't terribly shocking—I'm going to tell them exactly what they want to hear." She could see the muscles in Jed's jaws tighten.

Quickly she reassured him. "I'm not talking about a permanent arrangement, Jed," she said. As she spoke, she saw the tightness lessen slightly. She pulled him closer to her. Lightly, she stroked her finger along the hard muscles of his upper arms while dropping her voice to a warm intimate tone. "I want to be back in New York with you as soon as possible. You know that."

"Yes, I know," Jed answered. Wrapping his arms more tightly around her, he lowered his head and gently kissed her. Thoughts of Ryan Mining fled from Caitlin's mind, and all she could concentrate on was being secure in Jed's arms.

# 5

The long line of cars that formed the funeral procession wound slowly through the town toward the cemetery. It was a very old cemetery, with wide, sloping lawns and stately shade trees. According to her wishes, Mrs. Ryan would be buried between her late husband and her beloved daughter, Laura.

Melanie, riding in the limousine with Caitlin, thought about death and gave a little shiver. She glanced briefly at Caitlin, who was sitting beside her, and wondered what her thoughts were at the moment. She really had to hand it to Caitlin. Her future sister-in-law had handled the last few days with a lot more dignity than Melanie knew she would have been able to muster. Even when those clowns from the press had pushed forward, wanting to know how she was feeling about coming into so much power and money, Caitlin hadn't flinched. She hadn't so much as acknowledged their presence. Instead she walked straight to the car that was waiting for them. Despite being slightly pale, she still looked beautiful and calm in her black linen suit and black-veiled hat. Jed, in a dark blue suit, had done his best to shield her from people, stopping photographers from snapping her picture. Thankfully, no one would be allowed near them as they gathered beside the grave for the final goodbye.

They were now crossing through the huge, iron gates. The hearse had already turned in and was starting up the road that led to the grave site. At the top of the rise, the car stopped and the driver got out and held the door for them. Melanie walked ahead of the others to the row of green canvas chairs that had been set up beside the grave. As Jed, and Caitlin, and her father came up and sat down, Melanie noticed that Caitlin had taken a black-bordered handkerchief from her purse and was clutching it tightly. Her head was turned to watch as the pallbearers brought the casket forward to set it on the frame above the open grave.

The rest of the cars had come to a stop, lining the low grassy bank next to the road.

Melanie could hear the quiet, respectful murmurs of the guests as they began to gather around. There was a slight hush, then the minister began to read the final prayer.

Melanie tried to listen to the words, but soon her mind began to wander. She looked around at the other mourners, wondering if they were as bored as she was. Glancing over the casket at the people gathered on the other side, she thought she saw a familiar face. *No, it couldn't be.*

But it was. Laurence Baxter was standing across from her, dressed in a dark navy summer-weight suit. Seeing him sent an unexpected thrill through her. Suddenly it was as if the two of them were completely alone, all the other people around them faded into the distance. For a long time her eyes held his gaze. She couldn't seem to break away—and she didn't want to.

Then the spell was over, broken by the end of the service. Dr. Westlake stepped in front of Melanie to greet someone, and the others began moving away, too. When they moved out of her way, she looked where Laurence had been standing. He was gone.

She stood up. Not really knowing what to do next, she began to walk back down the hill toward the car. And then suddenly he was there, beside her, walking with her. He took her elbow. She could feel his hand, strong and warm, through the material of her dress.

"We have to talk," he said.

"No," she said firmly, determined not to let her true feelings for Laurence show. "There's nothing to talk about."

"You don't really feel that way," he replied. "Or you wouldn't have looked at me the way you did." He stopped her, grasped her shoulders and turned her toward him. "How long are you going to be here?"

"Until the end of the week," she said, her voice cracking even though she was trying desperately to stay cool.

"At nine o'clock tomorrow morning, I'll be waiting for you at the entrance of the estate."

"I won't be there," she insisted.

But he didn't wait for a response. He was already walking down the hill to his car. She saw it far along the line, a black convertible. Melanie watched as he got in and drove away.

She was not going to meet him the next morning. No matter what!

On Tuesday morning Caitlin's first priority was the meeting at Ryan Mining. Driving her grandmother's silver Mercedes, she had almost reached the main road when she noticed a car pulling away from the estate entrance.

She wondered about it briefly. Who was it, and what were they doing there? The car even looked a little familiar, but she couldn't place it. She couldn't tell who the two people inside were, either. They were just too far away. *Oh, well*, she thought, dismissing them. They were probably just stopping to check a map or something. People got lost on the back road near Ryan Acres all the time.

When she arrived at Ryan Mining, Caitlin stopped at the gate. Seeing the startled look on the guard's face, she realized he must have recognized the car and thought he was seeing a ghost. Pulling up beside the guard house, she smiled and said good morning. The guard's face relaxed as soon as he saw who it was. He lifted the gate and Caitlin drove in, parking in the space that had always been reserved for her grandmother.

The three men she had met with on Sunday were waiting for Caitlin in her grandmother's elegant office. They waited for her to cross the thick carpeting and sit down behind the antique mahogany desk. Her heart was hammering in her chest. She had dressed simply in a beige, raw-silk suit and an off-white blouse. Her only jewelry was a pair of gold earrings and her Cartier tank watch.

"All right, gentlemen," she said. "If you'll please be seated, we can start the meeting."

They sat down on the couch across from her, and Caitlin began. "I know you're eager to hear my decision, and I won't keep you waiting. I've decided to accept your offer of the presidency of Ryan Mining, but I must tell you, I'll depend on your experience and judgment enormously."

"Of course," Mr. Woods replied. "We'll do whatever we can." The others nodded in agreement.

"I do not, however, intend to be a figurehead," she went on. "While I'll need your input, from now on all major decisions affecting Ryan Mining will be made by me. Is that clear?" Caitlin's voice was firm, but her hands were trembling with nervousness. She hoped she looked more confident than she felt.

Mr. Gottlieb was the first to speak. "Certainly, Ms. Ryan. We'll do whatever we can to help during the transition."

"Yes," Mr. Woods agreed. "You have our complete support."

"Thank you," Caitlin replied. It looked as though she had passed the first test, anyway. "Now, let's get down to business."

It was nearly one o'clock in the afternoon when Caitlin returned to Ryan Acres. Feeling completely drained, she went into the library and with a heavy sigh, slumped down onto the couch. Kicking off her shoes, Caitlin leaned her head back and looked up at the portrait of her grandmother that hung over the mantelpiece. She smiled wryly. "Well, it looks like you have what you've always wanted—me as president of Ryan Mining."

"Caitlin?" Melanie called from the open doorway. "Is that you? Did I hear you talking to someone?" She came into the room and looked around at the empty chairs.

"Just to myself," Caitlin said, "I'm just tired, that's all."

"Pretty tough meeting, huh?" Melanie commented sympathetically. She came over and sat down beside Caitlin on the couch.

"Worse! I am now officially the president of Ryan Mining. This morning, I was voted in by the board of directors."

"Wow," Melanie gasped in amazement. For a long minute she stared through the french doors at the well-manicured lawn and the flower beds. Then she looked back at Caitlin. "How do they expect you to run Ryan Mining from New York?"

"They don't," Caitlin replied with a resigned toss of her head. "I'm going to have to stay here in Virginia. At least until I can find a new owner who will run the company the way I'd like to see it run."

"But what about Jed?" Melanie stared at her friend with a frown. "How do you think he'll take this?"

"He already knows. We talked about it before he went back to New York. He's not exactly thrilled about our being separated," she said with an unhappy shrug. "But it won't be for very long, a few months at the most. And I'll plan my time so I can get up to the city on the weekends. He can come down here sometimes, too. New York really isn't that far away."

"Neither is your wedding," Melanie said, reminding Caitlin of something that was already very much on her mind.

"I know," Caitlin answered with a faraway look. At Melanie's words, she felt a small dark cloud of worry form in her mind. *Oh, please,* she pleaded silently, *don't let Ryan Mining spoil our wedding plans.* Aloud, she just said, "I wish we were already married."

"I understand how you feel," Melanie responded in all sincerity. But talking about Jed and Caitlin reminded Melanie of her meeting with Laurence that morning, and soon their problems were forgotten. A smile touched her mouth, and she turned her head so Caitlin wouldn't notice and ask about it. To think she'd almost decided against meeting him.

Driving over the sunny, country roads, he

had told her how miserable he had been since she went back to New York. He said that she was the only girl he loved, and he had asked her if they could start over again. Now Caitlin was handing her a way to make that happen.

Trying to look completely sincere, she turned back to Caitlin, "I've just gotten the best idea," she said smiling. "What if I moved down here with you while you have to be here. I could help out here at Ryan Acres—you know, take care of the little things you won't have time for. That way, you would have more time to take trips to New York to see Jed. I really love it here, and I'd keep you from missing Jed too much."

"Oh, Melanie, that sounds great," Caitlin agreed quickly. But almost immediately she shook her head. "No, that wouldn't be fair for you. How about your plans for fall. You must have decided on something—a trip, your master's, maybe a job?"

"No. Actually I haven't made any plans." *Except to be with Laurence as much as I can*, she added silently. She looked away from Caitlin momentarily, feeling a tug of guilt for being so secretive about her relationship with Laurence. But, she reminded herself, it was important to keep it a secret until he could find the right time to make a clean break with Nancy. She looked back at Caitlin. "To be honest, I sometimes get tired of being cooped up in New York. It's a super place to live, don't get me wrong. But sometimes I really miss the open spaces of the country." She waved her hands as if to encompass the entire estate. "If I stayed, I could even get in some riding. And I'd like to try hunting. And I do like the friends of yours I've met so far, and—"

"Okay, okay," Caitlin said with a laugh. "You've convinced me. How soon do you want to move down here?"

"As soon as possible," Melanie replied breezily.

A few minutes later she left the library to go upstairs and pack an overnight bag. She decided it would be best to go to New York in person to make the necessary arrangements for her extended stay at the estate.

As soon as she had left, Caitlin went to the phone. There were two calls she had to make. The first person she had to call was Arlene, her editor at *National News*. Caitlin spoke quickly after she said hello, breaking the news that she would not be able to return to the magazine. "I think it only fair since I can't really be sure how long all this is going to take that I give you my resignation. I'm so sorry, but this situation has turned out to be more complicated than I'd anticipated."

"Oh, Caitlin, of course I understand," Arlene assured her sympathetically. But Caitlin could tell from her tone that Arlene was very disappointed. "It's just that—well, I really hate losing one of my best writers."

"Thank you." Then she added, "And thanks for everything else, too."

"It was my pleasure," she said and then paused. "Look, if you ever decide to stop being a business mogul, you're welcome back here anytime."

The two women talked for another few minutes, with Caitlin promising to have lunch with Arlene the next time she was in New York. Then, with a lump forming in her throat, Caitlin said goodbye. After breaking the connection, she prepared to make the next call to Jed.

"Hi," she said softly when he picked up. "I'm back from the meeting."

"And?"

"I said I'd do it," she said simply.

"Umm-hmm." He paused and she could hear a muffled sigh at the other end of the line. "You know, things don't look so bad now that I've had time to think about it and get used to the situation. I guess what I mean is, I think you're doing the right thing. So," he went on, "while I'm definitely not turning handsprings over the situation, I'll live."

"And I promise we'll be together every

weekend. I won't let anything interfere with our time together. In fact, I'm planning to come up there on Saturday. My apartment has to be closed up temporarily, and I have to decide what clothes I want to bring back here, and—"

"Not too many, I hope," Jed broke in. "Just enough for a short stay."

"Agreed," she said, nodding into the phone. "Anyway, as I was about to say, it'll only take a couple of hours to do that. Then I'll be yours for the rest of the day"—she dropped her voice to a low, intimate tone— "and the evening."

"A long evening?" Jed's tone matched hers.

"Definitely a long one," she answered, and this time smiled into the phone.

# 6

With tired eyes, Caitlin skimmed the rest of the report she had been reading, then tossed it onto the desk. Stretching her arms, she took a deep breath, then let it out slowly. She swiveled her leather executive chair about so that she was looking out of the window toward the Blue Ridge Mountains in the distance.

After her meeting with Mr. Woods on Tuesday, she had decided to spend the balance of the week going into the office every day. She had to teach herself about mining, and there was no reason not to start right away. Since then, she had spent hours reading the piles of reports and files Mrs. Stedman had brought her. Mrs. Stedman had worked for her grandmother for nearly twenty years, and she had promised to stay on as Caitlin's secretary.

Caitlin soon discovered there was a great

deal to absorb—and she had so little time. By Friday afternoon she felt she was finally getting a handle on what made the company run. And, while she was totally exhausted, it was a good kind of tired. It made her feel that she was doing her job well.

Looking out at the mountains in the distance, Caitlin thought about how different everything was back in New York. There were no grassy fields and open spaces—except in Central Park. If it weren't for the fact that she was going to be seeing Jed, she would almost hate to go back. It was strange, she mused, but she had never realized just how much a part of her the Virginia countryside was. It really was beautiful. Too bad . . .

She didn't finish the thought. It was dangerous to let herself start thinking that way. With a disapproving shake of her head, she reached for the report and again began studying the rows of figures.

Half an hour later she put the report down. She looked dejectedly at the tall stack of papers she still had to go over, then glanced at her watch.

She decided she would read them later that evening, perhaps after dinner. What she didn't finish that night, she could go over in the morning on the plane to New York. Standing, she reached behind her for her suit jacket.

A few minutes later, just as Caitlin was closing the clasps on her eelskin attaché case, Mrs. Stedman opened the door. "I'm so sorry, Ms. Ryan," she said apologetically, "but Mr. Woods wants to know if he can have a few minutes of your time. I tried to explain that you were about to leave for the day, but he insisted."

"It's all right, Grace," Caitlin said with a resigned sigh. "Tell him to come in." She smiled kindly. "And why don't you go on home now. It's been a long day."

"Thank you." The secretary returned the smile. "And you have a nice weekend in New York, Ms. Ryan."

"Sorry to disturb you, Caitlin," Randolph Woods said a moment later as he stepped into the office and closed the door behind him. "I promise I won't keep you too long."

Caitlin noticed the serious expression on his face. "This isn't bad news, is it?"

"No, no," he assured her, sinking into the comfortable leather chair in front of the desk. "Well, not exactly," he added, leaning forward earnestly. "I was wondering if it might be possible for you to postpone your trip to New York tomorrow—perhaps even put it off for a week?"

"Why?" she asked, looking directly at him. "What's happened?"

"Well, nothing yet," he said hesitantly.

"And, of course, the final decision is up to you. After all, you're the president of the company. It's just that—"

"Randolph! Please don't beat about the bush this way."

"All right." He took a deep breath and began to explain. "As you requested, I asked the public relations department to field all press inquiries about your taking over as president of the company. Everyone was told that you're just too busy at the moment to give any interviews. We even brought up the fact that you're still in mourning for your grandmother." He shifted uneasily in the chair. "It's apparently not enough. The people of the press are a demanding lot, and they won't let go of a story like this. I honestly can't blame them. It isn't every day that a very pretty, very young woman is named president of a major corporation."

"So you think I should call a press conference after all?"

"Yes." He nodded. "I don't see any other way, frankly."

"Oh, Randolph, I really hate publicity. Are you sure this is really necessary?"

"Caitlin, be realistic. At twenty-four, you're the youngest president of a major United States firm. Of course you're news."

"I guess you're right. All right," she said in

a resigned tone. "But it can wait until Monday, can't it? I've got plans for the weekend."

"Sorry. News is something that just doesn't wait. I'm being hounded to get you to hold a press conference tomorrow, and even if we could postpone it until Monday, we'd need you here to help with the preparations." He shrugged. "Now, do you want to do it here or at the estate? Wherever you say. Oh, also 'America In The Morning' is interested in having you come up to New York to be on the show sometime next week."

Caitlin was silent. Swiveling her chair around, she looked out the window for a long moment. She would have to call Jed, and she hated having to break the news to him. Well, at least she could tell him she would be in New York sometime later in the week to do the TV interview. They could be together then. He would just have to understand that things would be a little hectic for a while. Turning back to face the attorney, she sat up straight, and said, "All right, what do I have to do?"

The press conference was a smashing success, but it was also noisy, crowded, and exhausting. Caitlin had decided that the best place to hold it would be in her office. Dressed conservatively in a soft linen suit and white silk blouse, she met the reporters. Later, after the reporters and photographers and TV people had gone, Randolph turned to her. "You were wonderful, Caitlin. The press got the story they wanted, and I think you impressed everyone with your knowledge and intelligence." He chuckled. "And that pretty face didn't hurt, either."

The first releases went out on Monday, beginning with a lead story in the business section of *USA Today*, as well as stories in the *Wall Street Journal* and the Washington *Post*. *Time* and *Newsweek* magazines both planned to do feature articles on Caitlin that week. Of course, *National News*, the magazine Caitlin worked for, was preparing a big spread as well. Arlene called to say that the story would include a personal note from herself.

"I'm just going to share with our readers a few of my impressions of you—your spirit and intelligence," she said, with a smile in her voice. "I hope you don't mind."

"Thank you, Arlene. That sounds lovely. I hope to do my best for the company that was founded by my family."

She said the same thing to Sandy Hillman, the woman who interviewed her, when she appeared on "America In The Morning" on Tuesday morning.

"You know, Ms. Ryan, you really are quite young to be the head of such a large company," the woman said, leaning toward Caitlin. "At twenty-four, most young women are barely starting their climb up the corporate ladder. Do you honestly feel you're capable of taking on such a huge responsibility?"

"Yes," Caitlin replied instantly. Then looking directly into the camera, she said, "Actually the main reason I agreed to appear on your show was to assure everyone that I am quite capable. I don't go around seeking publicity," she added modestly. "I simply want to do the right thing for my company and, of course, my stockholders. I want them to have faith in me. And I want them to feel that that faith is justified." She looked back at Ms. Hillman with a charming smile.

They spoke for a few minutes longer, and then Ms. Hillman smiled thoughtfully. "I'll be watching for your name in the business news in the future. And I'd like to thank you for being our guest this morning." Pausing, she turned to face another camera. "We'll be back in a minute."

The red light on the front of the camera went out, and the director signaled they were off the air. Ms. Hillman rose to move to another section of the set. Before she left, though, she paused to shake Caitlin's hand. "It was a pleasure, really. Good luck in the future."

\* \* \*

Miles away in an expensively and tastefully decorated condo in the Washington D.C. suburb of Arlington, Virginia, Colin Wollman was watching "America In The Morning" along with several million other Americans. As the interview with Caitlin ended, he reached for the remote control and cut off the picture with an angry jab. His handsome, middle-aged face settled into a mask of hatred.

*Damn her! Damn Caitlin Ryan!* he swore softly. He sprang to his feet and strode across the living room, stopping in front of a beautifully lacquered Chinese cabinet. He stood for a moment debating with himself, then pulled open the doors to reveal a small, but fully stocked bar. Reaching for the bottle of scotch, he poured a generous amount into a glass, tossed it down, then poured some more. Feeling calmer, he carried the glass back to the leather couch and sat back down. After taking another sip, he put the glass down and distractedly ran a hand through his hair. He picked up the day-old copy of *USA Today* that was lying on the coffee table. It was folded open to the business page, and Caitlin's photograph stared back at him.

*Caitlin Ryan.* He hated her. How he despised that girl. If it hadn't been for her, a good deal of Regina Ryan's money would be his.

Reaching for the glass, he swallowed and thought back to the last time he had seen

Caitlin Ryan. He had had a scheme to "acquire" much of Regina Ryan's money. It was such a simple scheme, too, certainly simpler than most of the plans he had been involved in before. But that time, dear little Caitlin had ruined everything for him.

He had been working as an attorney in Washington, when he heard that the Ryan Mining attorney had died of a heart attack and that Regina Ryan was actively searching for someone to replace him. Knowing of Regina Ryan—and the Ryan fortune, of course—from the social pages, he decided to apply for the position, which would be useful in getting to know her better. With just a little luck, it wouldn't be long before he would be in a position to take control of her company—and her money.

Taking another swallow of scotch, Colin finished what was left in the glass. He got up and walked back to the cabinet. Sloshing more of the amber liquid into his glass, he went over to the window and stared down morosely at the snarl of early-morning traffic below. All those people on their way into the capital to start their workday, he mused, and there he was in his robe, drinking scotch. He just hadn't felt like going into the office that morning. And, now that he had seen Caitlin on TV, he definitely decided to stay at home.

As he watched her face, so animated and

self-confident, he had wanted to throw something at the TV. He wanted to break her the way she had broken him. Remembering the day she had faced him in the library at Ryan Acres to tell him she had enough information to have him arrested, he shook with anger. This wasn't supposed to have happened—no one should have caught him. Least of all Caitlin Ryan.

In the end Colin had run from Ryan Acres like a whipped dog with his tail between his legs. During the next few years he concentrated on building a new life for himself. Of course he had been disbarred, so he was no longer a lawyer. Instead he had become involved in real estate. Now he was welcome again at some of the nicer clubs and restaurants in town.

A pensive look crossed Colin's face, and his eyes narrowed. Oh, how he would love to see Caitlin Ryan squirm.

He took another swallow of scotch. As the liquor warmed his stomach a plan began to form in his mind. Perhaps, he thought, he might be able to arrange that. He hadn't been able to get the Ryan fortune, but what if he could arrange it so that Caitlin Ryan didn't get it, either? What if he could make sure she lost the company? What better revenge than to watch Ryan Mining go under right in front of

Caitlin's eyes. She wouldn't have the slightest inkling as to why—or who was behind it.

All that righteous slop she had spouted on "America In the Morning" about how she was going to carry on in the grand old Ryan tradition made Colin sick. But what if he could show that she was wrong, that her youth was a disadvantage after all? What if everyone thought she was nothing but a spoiled, rich, jet-setter who wanted to do nothing but party all the time? What if her stockholders suddenly began believing she was willing to give the company to anyone who would take it.

*Yes, yes,* he thought as a low chuckle formed in his throat. He could just imagine the stockholders rushing in droves to unload their shares of Ryan Mining. Caitlin wouldn't even know what was happening—and she would be absolutely powerless to stop it. All he had to do was start a few rumors in just the right places, and Colin did know those places. Throwing his head back, he laughed out loud. He could start the rumors circulating that very morning. With renewed energy, Colin turned and walked purposefully toward the phone. *Yes,* he thought with an evil smile, *Ryan Mining is all but history.*

# 7

Leaving the TV studio after saying goodbye to the producer, Caitlin stood on a corner to hail a cab to take her to her apartment on East Eighty-fourth Street. It was now eight-thirty, and she was meeting Jed at Luce's for lunch at noon. That gave her plenty of time to take care of the things she had to do.

A cab stopped and she climbed in, settling back against the worn upholstery. She made a list in her mind: first she would decide which clothes she would need in Virginia, then she would pack. And she wanted to box up some of the books she really treasured, as well as arrange to have a couple of her favorite paintings and prints shipped. She planned to hang the paintings in her office at Ryan Mining. Although she didn't intend to stay there a long time, Caitlin hated feeling as if the office still belonged to her grandmother. She had decided to put a few of her own things in it.

Caitlin glanced out of the cab window. They were moving so slowly. It was funny, she mused, how quickly she had forgotten about the terrible New York traffic.

Arriving at her building, she paid the driver, adding a good-size tip. He thanked her with a smile and a quick nod before driving away. The temperature was already climbing, and she hurried in to the building's air-conditioned lobby. But the elevator was stuffy, and so was her apartment as she let herself in. Caitlin was greeted by still, stale air and the slightly musty smell of an empty apartment. The flowers on the hall table had died.

Putting down her purse, she kicked off her shoes, flipped on her air conditioner and listened to it hum to be sure it was working properly. Then she carried the vase into the kitchen and disposed of the dead flowers. *Yuck*, she thought, opening the refrigerator and taking out a can of diet cola. She poured it into a glass, dumped some ice in, and carried it with her into the bedroom.

Changing from the suit she had worn for her interview into a pair of shorts and a T-shirt, she went to work. She tossed clothes out of the closet and onto the bed. Next came her lingerie and accessories from the dresser drawers.

By eleven o'clock she had packed five suitcases and put them beside the front door, ready to be picked up to be taken to the airport. A woman from an art gallery had come and picked up her Tissot oil, her Klinger and Renoir etchings, and her small Rodenbury sculpture, promising to have them delivered to Caitlin at her office on Thursday afternoon. All she needed to do was stop and talk to the superintendent on her way out. She wanted to ask if he could keep an eye on her apartment while she was gone. There was just enough time before she had to leave to take a shower and refresh her makeup so she would look beautiful for Jed.

Luce's was a small publike restaurant near Jed's office. Caitlin had always liked its casual atmosphere—sawdust on the floor, thick wooden booths, and gleaming brass trim on everything from the little lamps above each table to the coat hooks. She and Jed had met there for lunch often when she had worked at the magazine.

He was waiting for her, looking marvelously handsome. The collar of his white shirt was crisp and when he leaned down to kiss her hello, she caught the scent of the woodsy after-shave he used.

The hostess led them to a corner table, handed them menu cards, then left. Caitlin studied hers for a moment, then put it down. "I don't know why I bother looking. I know this thing by heart."

"Me, too," Jed said with a smile as he put his menu down as well. He looked away from her for a moment, collecting himself, then he looked back at her. "I went into the office a little late this morning so I could catch your interview."

"Good," she said. She shot him a questioning look. "At least I think so. Will you tell me honestly how you think I came across? All I've received so far are flattering comments—Melanie called, and so did Randolph Woods. Nice, but not exactly helpful."

"Well, to tell you the truth—" Jed was cut off in midsentence as their waiter came over to take their orders.

Caitlin leaned toward Jed after the waiter had left. "Was I that terrible? Really, you can tell me if I was."

"No—no," Jed replied quickly, shaking his head. "Of course not. I was a little bothered about *what* you said, but certainly not how you said it. You had me convinced—too convinced." Leaning back in his chair, he studied her face. "From the way you talked, it sounded as if you had made up your mind to stay on as president of Ryan Mining permanently. Was that solely for the benefit of any nervous stockholders who might have tuned in? Or have you changed your mind since the last time we talked?"

"Jed—" Caitlin began to explain.

"Look, I'm not trying to put you on the spot. It's just that what you said worried me. I know you must feel at loose ends, after giving up your job at *National* and all. But I hope all that guilt your grandmother heaped on you"—he shook his head—"no, I just hope you aren't making a mistake."

"Of course not, Jed. If you'd just let me talk—" Caitlin said. "Even though I'm not going to, I had to make it sound as if I plan to remain with the company. Naturally I had to be convincing." She paused. "And I do believe what I said. I do care about the company. That doesn't mean I intend to stay on forever, but I am a Ryan and I feel a certain responsibility toward Ryan Mining."

"I know you do. Just don't forget that pretty soon you'll be my wife, and you'll have a different set of loyalties. We decided our lives are going to be here in New York, remember?"

"Yes, Jed, of course I remember." She looked into the depth of his green eyes and saw the very real concern mirrored in them. "And I can't think of anything I want more, darling. I'm certain by the time we're married, everything will have been taken care of, and, perhaps, someone will have stepped forward to buy the company by then. Someone who will run the company the way it should be run."

"Wait, wait. What do you mean, the way it should be run?" Jed asked, looking puzzled. "From what I've heard, the company's been turning a handsome profit for years."

"Jed!" Caitlin put down the fork she'd been holding. "Surely you haven't forgotten about the terrible things we found out about the mines when we went to Rock Ridge that summer. That's Ryan Mining's responsibility—*my* responsibility."

Caitlin thought back to the summer she and Jed had helped to found a play school for the children of miners in a small, West Virginia town. They had discovered that some of the working conditions were quite dangerous. There had also been an aborted attempt at strip mining, which had left the formerly beautiful, wooded hills bare and ugly. Caitlin and Jed had promised the people in Rock Ridge that they would do whatever they could to change things and make them right. Unfortunately, no one had really listened to them, and the mines were almost as dangerous as ever.

"Well, of course, I haven't forgotten about that summer," Jed answered with a slight frown. "I guess—I guess I just assumed that some of those problems had been taken care of since you hadn't mentioned them again."

"All right, a couple of things were done— the equipment was updated, and the shifts were shortened. But there are still a lot of things I'd like to see changed. And now that I've got the chance to fix them, I'm going to take it."

"I don't know," Jed persisted. His lunch had just arrived and he picked up his fork. "It sounds to me as if you want to get involved. At first you said you just wanted to stay on until you could turn over the company—"

"Not just to anyone," Caitlin interrupted. She was feeling slightly perturbed. Why couldn't Jed understand? He had been as disturbed as she had been about the shameful conditions out at Rock Ridge. True, they hadn't discussed them in a long time, but he was acting as if the unsafe mines no longer mattered. Well, to her they did. "I don't want to turn over the company until all the injustices and hazards are completely abolished. That way, there will be a better chance they won't be repeated. And I want the company to go to someone who is going to care about the people who work for Ryan Mining." Caitlin's voice had grown louder. Suddenly she realized just how much, and she stopped talking. Taking her napkin from her lap, she dabbed at the corners of her lips, then draped it across her knee again. Calm once more, she looked across at Jed. She loved him so much, and she knew he was just concerned about her and about their lives together. "I'm sorry," she apologized. "That's the kind of speech I should be saving for the board of directors."

"Yes, well, I'm sure you'll have their complete attention when you talk to them that way." He smiled, but the tense look around his eyes was still there. She really was sorry, not because of her convictions about making changes at Ryan Mining, but because their time together was so brief. She didn't want to spend it arguing. Obviously Jed felt the same way.

"Hey," he said, leaning toward her. "Let's talk about something else, okay?" He glanced at his watch. "I'll have to leave in another twenty minutes." They spoke of friends and business for a while. Then finally Jed asked, "So how's Melanie doing? Is she helping at all?"

"Oh, absolutely," Caitlin replied. "I'm really glad she decided to stay at Ryan Acres."

"Good." Jed nodded. "Truthfully, I was

afraid she'd be bored and you'd end up having to find something to keep her busy."

"Well, it's only been a little more than a week, but already she's been doing a lot for me. Answering mail I can't get to, screening calls at home, making sure that the household runs smoothly. She's also been choosing menus and selecting flowers for the house arrangements, too—both things I don't have time to do myself."

Caitlin paused as the waiter came over and handed the check to Jed. He took a credit card from his wallet and handed it back. After the waiter had gone, Caitlin went on. "She's even found time for a new hobby, antiquing. Can you believe it? Maybe it's the Virginia country-side that did it to her, but I never thought she was the type. She went off in the morning a couple of times so far. When she came home, she was very excited about the things she had found."

"Melanie? That's hard to believe. What kind of things is she buying? Not furniture, I hope."

"No, mostly miniatures and candlesticks, that kind of stuff." The waiter returned. While Jed signed the credit slip, Caitlin continued to think about Melanie. She was glad that Jed's sister had found a new hobby. She had been worried that Melanie would have so much spare time that she would get involved with Laurence Baxter again. And Caitlin didn't want to have to nurse her through another unhappy scene. No, antiques were much safer. And Melanie would find the right man eventually. Laurence just wasn't the one.

Jed put the credit slip in his pocket. "I'll have to ask her to show me what she's bought when I come down this weekend."

He spoke so casually that it took Caitlin a moment to realize what he had said. Then she looked over at him in happy surprise. "Oh, Jed!" she cried. "How come you didn't say so right away? And how did you get the time off?"

"I got the okay last night," he said with a grin. He stood and came around to her side of the table to help her up. "The client I was going to have to work with on Saturday won't be coming to New York until next week."

"Oh, Jed, that's wonderful."

"I'll tell you what I think is wonderful," he said lowering his head so that his mouth was close to her ear. "Being alone with you on the terrace at Ryan Acres with the moon overhead and my arms around you. And I'll be able to kiss you for as long as I like."

"Ummm—" She smiled as he nuzzled her neck briefly before she bent to pick up her purse from where it lay on the table. "How about as long as I like?"

"Oh, yeah," he growled. Then he straightened up, and looking very proper they left the restaurant.

That evening over dinner Caitlin told Melanie about her lunch with Jed. "I'm so glad he's going to be able to come down for the weekend after all," she said after eating the last spoonful of Mrs. Crowley's wonderful vichyssoise. "I told him about your new interest in antiquing. Then I remembered that you'd said you were thinking about going down to Albemarle County this weekend to check out a place you'd heard about." She smiled across the table at Melanie. "I thought it would be fun if we all went together. We could even have lunch at that darling little inn near Monticello. There's a little place nearby that you should go see. Ginny Brookes bought a couple of things there that—" She paused, noticing the odd expression on Melanie's face. If she hadn't known better, she would have said it was a stricken look. "Melanie?" she asked, leaning forward. "Is something wrong? Are you feeling all right?"

"No, no, it's nothing, really." Melanie shook her head. But she didn't look as if she were telling the complete truth. "The cold soup hit a tooth that's been bothering me, that's all."

"Oh!" Caitlin nodded. "Well, if you're sure that's all it is."

"I'm sure," Melanie said, glancing down at her soup bowl. *Darn!* Now what was she supposed to do? She and Laurence had planned such a wonderful day for Saturday, and now Caitlin was messing everything up. Her antique-hunting story had worked so well to now. Caitlin hadn't even questioned the hours she had spent supposedly tracking down eighteenth-century candlesticks—except to ask if she had had a good time. But now it looked as though her date was off. She would have to call Laurence.

Glancing back up, she saw Caitlin was still watching her. She forced a smile. "I'd love to have you and Jed come along on Saturday. We'll have a great time."

# 8

Because of Jed's promise to visit that weekend, Caitlin went to the office the following morning in a happy, upbeat mood.

After giving Mrs. Stedman a list of the people she wanted to see, she began tackling the work on her desk. After conferring with the company engineers, she started the plans for turning a hilly area—gutted by strip-mining efforts—into a wooded park. When completed, the park would be given to the state. She then outlined her plans for the new inspection routine the miners were to follow. She wanted to be sure that shoddy inspections would never again be an excuse for the continued use of outdated or defective equipment. Then later she spoke with a representative of the West Virginia county where Rock

Ridge was located to see if it was possible to have the town's main street paved.

By Thursday she was feeling good about everything she had accomplished. She had even contacted the interior decorator Jed's cousin Emily had recommended and asked him to redecorate her office.

When she returned from a long lunch at three o'clock, she learned that the designer had been by and left the plans for the redecorated office. Gone would be the dark paintings of her grandmother as well as her leather chairs. They would be replaced by comfortable overstuffed chairs in tones of peach and dark green. The colors were to be taken from the large Tissot painting, which would hang behind her desk. The delicate Renoir and fantasy Klinger etchings would lighten the deep beige wallpaper, and the abstract, glass sculpture by Rodenbury would sit on a table between two windows, where it would catch and reflect the soft tree-filtered light from outside.

Caitlin was delighted with the design. Happy because everything seemed to be going so well, she decided to call Jed. She needed to know what time he planned to arrive the following day. And, besides, she still hadn't told him about her idea to go to Charlottesville with Melanie.

Sitting down at her desk, she picked up the

phone and dialed his office in New York. A few minutes later she was put through.

"Hi, Jed. I know I really shouldn't be bothering you at the office, but I just had to talk to you and hear your voice."

"I—I'm glad you did," he said. But as Jed spoke, she heard the hesitation in his voice.

"Jed, is something wrong?" she asked quickly.

"Not really. It's just that I'm going to have to cancel our plans for this weekend," he said. "Now I've got to be here for a different client. I'm really sorry."

"Oh, no! You're kidding," Caitlin replied, feeling terribly disappointed. "Jed, that's not fair. Tell that client you already have plans."

"Come on, you know that I can't do that," Jed said softly. "But what about you? Can you come up here? I won't have to be with the client long. We could go out later—maybe even to Chin's in the Village or to that great Italian place near you. Better yet, we could order a pizza and spend the evening at my place."

"Oh, Jed, you know I'd like nothing better," Caitlin said with a sigh. "But I can't come up there. You know I can't."

"Yeah," Jed said in a disgruntled tone. "I know. You're not supposed to be away from the company at this time. My God, you'd think it was a baby instead of a coal-mining company."

"Jed, be fair. This is a difficult time at Ryan Mining."

"You just finished saying everything is great," he retorted sharply. "You've got all these projects going. When they hear about what you're doing, your employees should turn handsprings. What more can you ask for?"

She paused for a long moment before answering. Then she lowered her voice and said seriously, "You here with me, Jed darling. That's what else I'd like."

"I wish I could make it, honest. But you know I'll be thinking about you. I'll call tomorrow night, okay?" He paused, and it sounded as if he'd put his hand over the mouthpiece. When he spoke again, it was in a hurried, businesslike voice. "I'm sorry, Caitlin, I've got to go. I'll call you later, promise." He hung up before she had even had a chance to say a real goodbye. But even though she felt disappointed, she understood how business could rule one's life. Ryan Mining business was certainly ruling hers. Understanding didn't make things better, though.

Caitlin didn't have time to dwell on thoughts of Jed. Just as she had opened a file on her desk, she was interrupted. The door to her office burst open, and Randolph Woods unceremoniously rushed in. Letting the file drop, she looked up at him with startled concern. "What is it Randolph?"

The young lawyer strode directly to her desk. Setting his fingertips on the top, he leaned toward Caitlin, looking her grimly in the eye. "Caitlin, we've got problems." She looked back at him evenly, and he went on. "Since the opening of the stock market this morning, we're down five and a half points," he answered.

"What are you talking about, Randolph?" Caitlin suddenly felt as though a hand were about to close around her throat. "You said only yesterday that the price of our stock had risen one and a half points per share this week."

"I know." He straightened up and pushed his hand through his wavy hair. "And for Ryan Mining, that's good—even excellent. We've always been a steady stock. But this—"

"All right," Caitlin said, forcing herself to think calmly. "What's causing this run on the stock? Do you have any idea?"

"We're not sure. I've had my people working on the problem since I was first told of it this morning. One of the board members, who's on the exchange, called to let me know a rash of selling had started right after the doors opened this morning," he explained.

"This morning!" Astonished, Caitlin stood and glared at her attorney. "Why wasn't I told immediately?"

"Well—" the attorney began, looking slightly sheepish. "I didn't want to bother you. You've been so busy, working on all those projects of yours."

Caitlin continued to stare at him for a long moment, then with a shake of her head, she walked to a window and stared out, her hands on her hips. Finally she turned. "Randolph, I really don't believe you just said that. I thought you, of all people, understood me— how serious I am about running this company."

"I know—I know," Randolph said. "But you are new, and I thought I could take care of it without having to trouble you. But when I got the final figures when the market closed today, I knew I'd better come to you. I'm sorry," he said, apologizing. "It won't happen again."

"All right, Randolph. It's okay." She sighed and walked back to her desk. "So what have you done so far?" She sat down again, resting her hands in her lap, and looked at him.

"Well, we know this much. There've been some rumors circulating. We don't know exactly what, each one we've heard is slightly different. But basically they all say that you're incompetent. People are saying that you really are too young—that you're playing at being the president of the company."

"How can we stop this?"

"It's hard." The attorney shook his head gravely. "I saw this sort of thing happen once before, and it may mean someone is attempting to take over the company. I hate to be the bearer of bad news, but—"

"Then don't!" Caitlin gripped the arms of her chair. She rose again. "I'm in charge, and this is my company. I am not going to watch it be destroyed."

"What are you going to do?" The attorney looked at Caitlin, impressed by her strength of character.

"I don't know, Randolph." She took a deep breath, then let it out. "Something." She glanced at her watch. "The market's been closed for an hour, and it won't open again until tomorrow morning. That gives me some time. Now, if you don't mind, I'd like to be alone to think."

As the door closed behind Randolph, Caitlin sank back down into her chair. Lines of worry appeared between her eyebrows. She glanced at the phone, wanting to pick it up and call Jed to ask him what she should do. She even reached for it once, but then dropped her hand back onto her desk. She knew all too well what he thought about her involvement in Ryan Mining. He'd probably tell her to sell before anything else happened. But she couldn't do that. She was a Ryan, and a Ryan didn't run from a fight. And this was definitely a fight.

But she did need help. She needed advice. But who to turn to?

Of course. Why hadn't it occurred to her sooner? Turning her chair back to face the desk, she reached out and picked up the phone. Dialing, she crossed her fingers and hoped her father would be in.

"Hi, I'm so glad I caught you in your office. I need some advice. Do you have a few minutes?"

"For you, honey, anytime," her father said in a kind tone. Then he paused. "From the tone of your voice, it sounds as though something's really wrong. How can I help?"

"My attorney has just told me that the price of Ryan Mining stock is slipping badly—and it all happened since this morning."

"Oh, dear. That does sound serious. Do you have any idea why the price is falling so fast?"

"Randolph says some kind of rumors are being circulated about me—that I'm too young and I don't care what happens to Ryan Mining." She sighed. "I've tried so hard to do what's right."

"Of course, I know that, honey. Do you have any idea who's spreading the rumors?"

"No. That's what's so strange. Randolph says it sounds like some kind of takeover attempt."

"I think he might be right."

"Really? Then what am I going to do? I told Randolph I'd handle it, but I'm honestly not sure how to go about it. That's why I called you."

She could hear him shuffling through some papers. "You know, Caitlin, I just might be able to help. A young man I know—his name's Howard Josso. He's an attorney. He was with Watham and Blodgett, but then he solved a takeover case that got a lot of media attention. That led to another firm asking for his help— and so on. Now that's all he does."

"Do you think he would be interested in helping me?"

"Yes—yes, I do. I think this might be just the kind of case he would find interesting. I'll tell you what, I'll hang up now and see if I can get ahold of him. He lives in Washington luckily. I'll tell him just what you've told me and see what he has to say."

"Thank you so much," Caitlin said. "I just knew I could count on you."

"Always, honey. And now I'll say goodbye. Call you as soon as I have some news."

Caitlin heard the click of the receiver on the other end. Slowly she also hung up. She was still concerned, but at least she had done something positive.

At dinner that night she told Melanie that Jed wouldn't be coming down for the weekend. "So I guess we'll have to cancel the trip to Albemarle County," she said apologetically. "I'm really sorry. Normally I'd say we could still go, but I'll probably be tied up all weekend with business."

"Of course, I understand," Melanie replied. "And I'm really sorry about what's happening with Ryan Mining. Don't even give a thought to me. I'll just go ahead by myself—get out of your hair, if nothing else," she said thoughtfully. "After all, I'd planned to go alone in the first place." *Well, not exactly alone,* she thought, trying not to smile in front of Caitlin. Now she could call Laurence and tell him their Saturday plans were on again.

Caitlin, still distracted by her problems, should have seen the sudden sparkle that appeared in Melanie's eyes, but she didn't.

It was almost ten when her father called. She took it in the library. "I've contacted

Howard Josso," he said. "He sounded intrigued by the situation and has agreed to talk to you about it."

"Intrigued?" Caitlin repeated. "What's this guy like? You make it sound as though he's some sort of mysterious hero, straight out of a TV movie."

"Not quite," Dr. Westlake replied, chuckling at her description despite the seriousness of the situation. "He's brilliant, young, about thirty. He really does nothing but help fight company takeovers now. When I told him about your situation, he said it sounds to him as if someone is trying to undermine you so they can pick up the company cheap when you're forced to sell. Also, he doesn't just take on any company that's in trouble. He only takes cases he feels are a real challenge."

"And he thinks Ryan Mining will be a challenge? That sounds like it's going to be a real fight to keep the company from going under," Caitlin said worriedly. "I don't like the sound of it."

"I think he also likes what he's heard and read about you," Dr. Westlake said.

"Oh?" Caitlin was surprised.

"He's heard what you've tried to do in just the past two weeks, and he admires you. And frankly, honey, I feel the same way. Of course,

I'm just a proud father, so it's nice to hear that an outsider feels the same way."

"Thanks."

"At any rate, he'll be at your office at eleven-thirty tomorrow morning. I said you'd call if the time's a problem."

"This man sounds like just what I need," Caitlin said. "You'd better believe I'll be free to see him. In fact, I'll cancel all my appointments for the day. He'll have my full attention."

"Excellent," Dr. Westlake replied. "That's just about what I told him." He chuckled softly again. "I know my daughter pretty well." His voice turned serious. "And I also know that you're a fighter. You're going to come out of this just fine, I know it."

"Thank you. With you behind me, how can I lose?" She smiled into the phone. "I love you."

"I love you, too, honey. Good night, sweet dreams now. Everything's going to be all right. Promise."

But as she hung up the phone, she couldn't help wondering if it really would be. Apparently it would all depend on Howard Josso.

## 9

At quarter to eleven the following morning, Melanie watched from one of the front windows as Caitlin drove away. She had said something at breakfast about an important meeting and that she was feeling slightly nervous. But to Melanie, Caitlin looked very cool and in complete control of herself—as usual. She was dressed in a lime green silk dress, with her dark hair swept up from her neck in a simple twist.

Melanie glanced down at her own casual clothes—shorts and a flowered shirt. While she didn't think she'd ever be as elegantly sophisticated as Caitlin, she could at least do her best to look pretty for her lunch date with Laurence. So what if she wasn't like Caitlin. All that mattered was that Laurence thought she was pretty. And he did. He had even said so the week before when they went swimming at his club. He had said she reminded him of a young movie star whom she thought was beautiful. Well, you couldn't get much better than that, she decided with a smile.

She raced upstairs to go through her closet and pick out something that would set Laurence's pulses racing. The new pink linen dress she had just bought would be perfect! It showed off her figure and her tan. Happy, she turned and started down the hall toward her room. Where was he taking her? She tried to remember. It was someplace she had never been. Some Greek place, that was it. Oh, well, it didn't really matter. She would order a salad and then just pick at it the way she always did.

Howard Josso was on time, almost to the second. When he walked into her office and held out his hand, Caitlin's first thought was that she hadn't been far off the mark when she said to her father that he sounded like some sort of TV hero. He certainly looked like one.

She had cancelled all of her appointments that day, and now she was glad she had. In addition to the handsome blond exterior, she liked what she saw. He looked competent and serious—like someone she could trust with the fate of the company. Caitlin was prepared to sit down and spend the day with him. So she was a bit surprised when his first suggestion was that they leave the office.

"Let's talk over lunch," he said, reaching for her purse and handing it to her. Then he took her arm and steered her toward the door. "I know of a little Greek place. It's a bit far but I know you'll love it."

Caitlin nodded in agreement, and they left the office. It wasn't until they were in his car, a plush BMW, that he explained, "I thought someplace besides your office would be the best place to talk. People who appear to be the most loyal employees sometimes turn out to be the ones who cause these problems. Everyone has a price: a secretary who feels she should be living in a villa in Nice, a bookkeeper whose wife needs an operation—"

"I see," Caitlin said with a grim smile. She looked out the window at the passing scenery, not really seeing it.

At the restaurant they were seated at a table in an alcove not far from the front door. Howard was seated so that he had a view of the main dining area, and Caitlin noticed that, while he paid close attention to her, he also had a habit of searching the room with his eyes. Rather than bothering her, she found his

habit reassuring. He was obviously very ob-
servant.

Because Howard knew the restaurant well,
Caitlin suggested that he order for her. The
food—pasta salad with feta cheese, served
with flatbread warm from the oven—was delicious, but Caitlin barely tasted it. She was too
busy answering the questions the handsome
attorney was throwing at her. At first she
didn't think they were leading anywhere. His
questions seemed so random. Some of them
were about the company, some about her
grandmother, but most of them were about
herself and the people she knew growing up.
Then Howard explained that he needed to
know everything about her life and about
Ryan Mining. Even things that didn't seem
important.

Later, as Caitlin had just begun telling him
about Colin Wollman, Howard was distracted
by something, or someone, behind her. "Excuse me," he said, interrupting her. "There's a
pretty young woman headed our way, and she
looks nervous about something."

But as Caitlin swung around in her chair,
she saw only a smiling Melanie approaching.
"Melanie, hi! What a coincidence."

"Yes, isn't it?" she replied, clutching her
purse. "I—uh, I was just doing a little shopping. I got hungry and stopped in here for

lunch. I was just leaving when I spotted you and thought I'd better say hi so you wouldn't think I was being rude."

"I'm glad you did," Caitlin said and smiled. Then she gave her a puzzled look. "Where were you shopping around here?"

"Well, actually I'd heard about this restaurant," Melanie said with a nervous laugh. "And you know me—I love Greek food."

"Actually, I didn't know that. Oh," Caitlin added, turning to include Howard, "I'm being rude. Let me introduce you."

After brief introductions, Melanie excused herself and left, saying she'd see Caitlin at home later.

"That's odd," Caitlin said, looking back at Howard. "I can't imagine why Melanie would want to come here to have lunch by herself." She shrugged. "Oh, well. As I was saying, Colin Wollman was my grandmother's attorney."

While he was still listening to Caitlin, another part of Howard's mind was replaying what had just happened. Why had Melanie Michaels lied to Caitlin? And he was certain she had. He had seen her coming from the back of the dining room with a young man. He had had his arm around her, and they had been laughing about something. When Melanie had happened to glance in their direction, her happy expression had changed quickly to one of near panic. She had whispered something to the young man with her, and he hurried out the front door of the restaurant. She had then headed straight to their table. He wondered if it were possible that Melanie had anything to do with Caitlin's problem with Ryan Mining. It didn't seem likely, but the girl was doing something behind Caitlin's back. Yes, it was possible. But he had learned from experience that clients would get very touchy if he accused anyone close to them. So, he decided, it would be best not to say anything about what he had seen until he could find out more about this Melanie person. Satisfied, he returned his attention to Caitlin and what she was telling him about her grandmother's former attorney.

One of Caitlin's favorite activities had always been riding. She loved horses with an undying passion. So on Saturday morning, with nothing to do but stew over her problems, Caitlin decided to take Duster out. She knew he could use the exercise.

She quickly dressed in a pair of slim-fitting fawn breeches, polished black boots, and a cool, yellow cotton shirt. Brushing her hair back, she wove it into a single braid, then she picked up her hunt cap and went downstairs, through the house, out across the back lawn, and down to the stable. When she got there, she asked Jeff, the stable hand, to saddle the shiny black Thoroughbred for her.

Mounting Duster she could feel his muscles bunching, as if he, too, could hardly wait to gallop through the fields and into the woods. With a light laugh, she expertly gathered in the reins, and set her feet into the stirrups. "Easy, boy, you know the rule—we always walk the first mile out and the last mile in." Turning to Jeff, she said, "I'll be out for about three hours, so don't worry if I'm not back before then. I think Duster needs a real workout." Then, with a gentle squeeze of her knees, she allowed Duster to prance just a bit before making him settle down to a flat-footed walk. They headed toward the wooded hills behind the estate.

Leaving Ryan Acres earlier, Melanie had driven straight to her meeting with Laurence. They were going to play tennis, then have lunch at his apartment, so they wouldn't run into Caitlin. That moment at the restaurant had been horrible. She knew Caitlin hadn't spotted her, but that guy she was with certainly had—and he had given her a look that could have soured milk. It was as if he had seen right through her. Obviously he hadn't said anything to Caitlin about seeing her hustle Laurence out of the restaurant. If he had, Caitlin would definitely have said something. The question was why hadn't he? Well, whatever his reasons were, she had a gut instinct about Howard Josso. She just didn't like him. There was something too slick and handsome about him. He was cute, but he seemed to know it. He seemed to know everything.

All the sneaking around was getting to be too much for her anyway, Melanie was thinking as she pulled up to the parking area near the tennis courts. She decided that right after their game, she would tell Laurence that she didn't want any more deception. It was time for him to break things off with Nancy for good. Let her know she had been replaced. Good grief, how hard could that be, anyway.

But Melanie couldn't bring herself to talk about Nancy over lunch. Laurence had gone all out. Arriving back at his apartment feeling hot and tired from several sets of tennis in the warm August morning, she had taken a quick shower. Then she had changed into fresh slacks and a silk shirt and come out to find the table set with fresh flowers and Laurence's heavy blue and white china. A salad had been chilling in the refrigerator, and there was also a warm loaf of french bread, a wedge of Brie cheese, and a bottle of chilled white wine.

Melanie had kept the talk light, unable to ruin the beautiful meal. But later, when Laurence suggested they take a drive in the foothills of the Blue Ridge Mountains, she agreed quickly. It was the perfect opportunity to broach the subject.

She started off easily enough, bringing up the hassle of constantly looking for places where they wouldn't run into his or Nancy's friends. They were driving with the top down, and at first she didn't really notice how quiet he had become. After she mentioned how terrified she had been at the Greek restaurant Laurence's jaw began to tighten. Finally he pulled off to the side of the road, turned off the engine, and faced her.

They were on a side road, not too far from Ryan Acres. But Melanie wasn't worried that she'd be seen. The employees from the estate never used this road. It wasn't connected to the road that went by the entrance, so there was no danger Caitlin would drive by, either.

"Why do you have to spoil the day this way?" Laurence demanded, looking at her sharply. "I don't want to talk about Nancy."

"But I do!" Melanie said evenly. "And I think it's about time, too. You say you love me, but you also keep saying it isn't the right time to tell Nancy about us."

"It isn't really." Laurence put his hands on her shoulders and looked into her eyes. "I do love you. But, please, just let me talk to Nancy in my own way, in my own time."

"There's been plenty of time," she insisted, looking off into the distance. Then she turned back to him. "I can't help it, Laurence. I get the feeling you're stalling, that you have no intention of breaking things off with Nancy." She swallowed hard. "That you're just toying with me."

"No, Mel, you're wrong," Laurence exclaimed. "It's not that way at all." He held her shoulders and gently forced her to look at him while he explained that he just couldn't hurt Nancy that way—not just then.

Several minutes later she happily allowed him to pull her into his arms for a long, fervent kiss.

It was just at that moment that Caitlin happened to ride to the top of a nearby ridge. Drawing Duster to a halt, she leaned forward to pat his neck while he caught his breath. Looking down at the road below, she saw the black Mustang. With a sinking heart, she recognized the couple in the front seat. Quickly, before they could spot her, she gathered up her reins and turned Duster.

That evening as they sat on the terrace having a glass of white wine before dinner, Caitlin confronted Melanie.

"I know you've been seeing Laurence," she said in a gentle voice.

"Oh, come on," Melanie said. "Where did you hear that, Caitlin? I've been doing everything but see Laurence."

"Please don't lie, Melanie. And nobody told me. I happened to see you today. You were on the back road, parked in Laurence's convertible."

"What?" Melanie stared hard at Caitlin, then her face flamed an angry red. "You were spying on us weren't you? How dare you!"

"I wasn't spying," Caitlin said as she shook her head. "I was out riding, and I just happened to be in the wrong place at the wrong time. I wish I hadn't seen you two, but I did."

"Ohhh!" Melanie cried. Embarrassed by her outburst, she looked down at her drink. "I'm sorry," she said apologetically a moment later, looking up again. "I shouldn't have called you a spy. And I know, honestly, that you only have my best interests at heart." She took a deep breath and let it out slowly. "I also know just how terrible all this must look to you. In fact, I felt the same way. That's what I was talking to Laurence about this afternoon. That's what we were doing parked there."

"And what did he say?" Caitlin asked, her voice low and thoughtful.

"Oh, Caitlin—" Melanie began, looking relieved. "He explained everything to me. The reason he hasn't told Nancy about us yet is that she's going through a tough time right now. Her mother's really sick, and she's going to have this awful operation. She might even die," Melanie went on. "Laurence says he doesn't want to cause her any more pain by telling her they're through. He wants to wait. He says he'll break the news to Nancy after the operation." She smiled nervously. "So, you see, everything is going to work out fine."

"I see," Caitlin replied in a quiet tone. She didn't say anything for a long moment, running her finger lightly around the top of her frosty glass. Then she looked up. "Just be careful, Melanie. Don't give him all of your heart just yet," she warned.

"But, Caitlin—" Melanie's eyes were dreamy. "I already have."

# 10

Hoping that the price of Ryan Mining stock hadn't slipped any farther, Caitlin arrived at the office Monday morning to find her office had been completely redecorated and looked exactly as the drawing had. She was thrilled.

A few minutes later Randolph Woods joined her. Caitlin steeled herself for the worst and was surprised to hear him say, "Good news, Caitlin. We're down only half a point this morning. The plunge seems to be leveling off."

Caitlin slipped out of her suit jacket, then sat down in her chair behind the desk. Mrs. Stedman appeared a minute later with coffee for Caitlin and Randolph in delicate Sèvres cups and saucers. She then disappeared just as quickly and quietly as she had entered.

"That woman is absolutely wonderful," he commented as soon as the secretary had left the room. "If you should ever decide you don't need her, please let me be the first one to know she's available."

"I will," Caitlin promised him with a polite smile. "But don't count on it happening too soon." Shifting slightly in her chair, she rested her elbows on the desktop and looked at him thoughtfully. "Do you think this means the worst is over?"

"I hope so, but I doubt it. Perhaps your Mr. Josso is getting results already, but it may be only a lull in the storm."

"Well, thank you for being candid," Caitlin told him. "I guess all we can do now is wait."

"On that note, I think I'll leave you to your morning mail." He nodded toward the neat pile of envelopes on her desk.

The run on Ryan Mining stock, which had begun the week before, did indeed appear to be over. Still, there was a continual steady move downward, if only by a fraction of a point every day: five-eighths of a point by closing on Monday, half a point on Tuesday, another point on Wednesday. Caitlin knew that if it continued for very long, it could spell a financial disaster. And it would take months, maybe even years, for the company to recover. In fact, if the trend weren't stopped, it could very well mean the end of Ryan Mining.

Caitlin told Howard of her fears over dinner that Wednesday night. She had invited him to Ryan Acres thinking it would be easier to discuss the situation in the privacy of her own library than in some formal, unfamiliar restaurant.

Actually, despite the business reasons for the dinner, Caitlin found herself enjoying Howard's company. It was only the two of them—Melanie had openly admitted to having a date with Laurence. She had been on her way out when Howard arrived. Caitlin couldn't help but notice the somewhat strained greeting the two had exchanged. She wondered briefly why they were both so distant. They barely knew each other. What could possibly be wrong between them?

Because of the warm weather, Caitlin had asked Mrs. Crowley to prepare a light meal of cold crabmeat and salmon with fresh fruit for dessert. They ate on the terrace as the sun was setting behind the trees. Rollins had lit the candles in the hurricane lamps, and they cast a restful glow on the table.

Howard looked like a young Robert Redford. Dressed in slacks, a tan linen jacket, and a light blue shirt, he was very handsome. And their conversation was not limited to business. Caitlin soon discovered that Howard was interested in jazz as well as contemporary literature, both favorite subjects of hers.

After dinner they went into the library, where coffee was served. In the more businesslike atmosphere, Howard retrieved his notes from his briefcase, and they settled down on the sofa to go over them.

"What I've done so far," he told her, setting a page before her on the coffee table, "is to eliminate the weaker possibilities. I can't narrow it down very far yet. He or she might be someone very close to you or a perfect stranger—I just can't tell yet."

"Oh, Howard, I can't believe it's anyone I know. I just can't," she said, shaking her head. "What makes you think it might be, anyway?"

"Because some of the rumors—and this is why they are being so readily accepted—deal with the kind of things it could be hard for a stranger to find out. But people who know you, well—they could find out your secrets."

"What secrets?" she asked, astonished.

"The fact that your grandmother opposed your relationship with Jed Michaels. They're saying he's after your money. There's also the accident in which a little boy was temporarily paralyzed. I know you were only in high school, and you did make amends, but you were still at fault. I'm afraid it doesn't make you look terribly responsible." He stopped speaking as a stricken look passed over Caitlin's face.

"Stop, don't say anymore," she said in a strangled voice. "How could anyone do something so awful?"

"I know. It's vicious," Howard agreed. "Unfortunately, this is the kind of thing I see all the time." He put a comforting hand on her shoulder. "But I am getting closer to the person who's spreading these rumors. And I promise that I won't stop until I find who it is."

"Thank you. Thank you so much, Howard," she said softly, with a grateful smile. "I really am counting on you."

"And I won't let you down," he said. He meant it with all his heart, too. In the short time he had known Caitlin Ryan, he had come to respect her enormously. No, he wouldn't let her down.


Before Caitlin went to bed that night, she called Jed. She just wanted to talk and let him know how Howard was coming along with the investigation.

Jed listened quietly while she spoke. He didn't interrupt her once, although he normally did during their phone talks.

"Well?" Caitlin asked when she finished telling him about the evening. "It sounds positive, don't you think?"

"Positive?" Jed's voice rose. "How can you call finding out some creep is out there spreading terrible gossip about you positive?"

"Not that part, Jed. I mean the fact that Howard's narrowing the list of suspects down. It won't be long before this is all over."

"I know how to stop it immediately," Jed put in. "Sell the blasted company. You're going to, anyway, so why not sell it now before the stock drops any lower? When the new owner takes over, the stock will probably climb right back up to where it was and the company will be fine."

"No! No, Jed, I won't do that. I know why you're saying this—because you don't want to see me hurt. But I can't walk away from this. I can't let people continue to believe those ugly exaggerations are all there is to Caitlin Ryan. I've got to stay and fight." She paused, then quietly added, "I don't think you'd be proud of me if I didn't."

"I'd be proud of you either way—either way takes guts," Jed replied solemnly. "Look, I'm sorry. I only want your happiness—our happiness." He sighed deeply. "If you feel you have to fight this, then I suppose you must."

They spoke for a few minutes more, then

said good night. After he hung up, Jed sat for a long time, thinking. He wasn't happy about the thoughts that whirled around his worried mind. He knew Howard Josso was a necessary person in Caitlin's life, and he told himself he shouldn't be jealous. Still, it bothered him to have another man—especially someone as handsome and brilliant as Caitlin said this guy was—spending so much time with Caitlin. He should be the one who was with her. No, it was definitely not the greatest situation. But what was really gnawing away at him was that, in her fight to save Ryan Mining, Caitlin seemed to be building a new life in Virginia—a life that didn't include him.

Although she felt exhausted when she crawled into bed, Caitlin had a restless night. Jed had tried to sound supportive on the phone, but his real feelings had come through clearly. It was obvious to her that he was beginning to resent the time she was spending at Ryan Acres. If only he could understand that she had meant it when she said she wasn't a quitter. She had to stay. Besides, she really did want to complete the changes she had begun. But what surprised her the most was the new understanding that was growing inside her, the understanding of how her grandmother had felt about the company. Caitlin now realized why her grandmother had wanted her to agree to take her place when she died. But that wasn't possible, even now. Ryan Mining still had no permanent place in her life—or did it?

Caitlin felt drained and exhausted the next morning as she arrived at work. Even Mrs. Stedman's excellent coffee didn't seem to revive her. What she really wanted to do, she thought, was go home, change into her riding clothes, and take Duster for a long ride.

Ironically, when she finally decided to tackle the stack of mail that was waiting for her, one of the first items she opened was a slick, full-color brochure for a nationally known yearling sale coming up the following weekend.

The brochure had been addressed to Regina Ryan, Caitlin noted, looking at the computer-printed label. Her grandmother had been the one who attended all the horse sales. She continued her interest in Thoroughbred breeding until the time of her first stroke. Since then, most of the breeding stock had been sold off. The ones that remained at the estate were family riding horses.

Leaving the rest of the mail to wait for a bit, Caitlin leaned back in her chair and began to flip through the pages. There was photo after photo of the best young horses available. At first she was only curious. What real interest could she have? she asked herself. You don't buy horses when you're planning to move back to New York City. But then she found herself staring at one particular horse, a stud colt. He was a real beauty, with a fine, sensitive head, conformation that showed the promise of speed, and intelligent eyes. She read the particulars listed beneath the picture. He had great bloodlines. It was all there. Oh, she would love a chance to bid on that one. "No, Caitlin," she said out loud to herself. Firmly closing the brochure, she set it aside. But then she tucked it into her briefcase—it couldn't hurt just to look at it.

She went back to the mail, disposing of most of it within half an hour. Near the bottom of the stack, she found a letter that made her smile.

It was an answer to a letter she had sent the week before, asking an old friend to lunch. Caitlin looked at the round, still somewhat childish handwriting on the front of the small envelope, then turned it over and quickly slit it open. As she took out the sheet of pale pink stationery, a picture of the young writer formed in her mind.

Little Kathy Stokes, with her wide gray eyes

and long dark hair was such a sweet little girl. She had been Caitlin's favorite student at the playschool she and Jed had helped establish in Rock Ridge. Caitlin had been amazed by the little girl's bright mind, and Kathy had followed her around adoringly. Once she admitted a little shyly that she thought there was only one other person in the world who was more super than Caitlin, her big brother. At the memory, an unhappy expression crossed Caitlin's face. Kathy's big brother was Julian Stokes—handsome, evil, cruel Julian Stokes. He had hated Caitlin since they were both children and she went to Rock Ridge with her grandmother to hand out Christmas presents. His pride had been hurt when she snubbed him, and he had never forgotten the incident. Later, when they were both students at Carleton Hill University, he planned a terrible revenge against her—and against Jed as well. With the help of Caitlin's roommate, Julian managed to break Caitlin and Jed up. Then he pretended he was in love with her himself. She thought she was in love with him, too. She had almost given herself to him completely, when the truth was uncovered. Julian pleaded with her to stay with him, telling her he had fallen deeply in love with her. But she could only feel disgust for him, and she had told him so before turning her back on him for good.

She loved Kathy, though. In the time since she had broken up with Julian she had come to admire the girl very much. And now Kathy was thirteen. Caitlin looked down at the letter.

I can't begin to tell you how excited I am about coming up there for lunch. I'm really looking forward to seeing you, Aunt Caitlin. I've even got a brand-new dress I'm planning to wear. Hope you like it.
Love, Kathy

She put the letter down. The lunch was to be the next day. She could hardly wait. Now that she knew Kathy was actually coming, Caitlin began to plan in her mind where she'd take the teenager. It had to be somewhere where the food was good and the atmosphere was fun, but not too intimidating for a young girl who had spent her whole life in a coal-mining town. Caitlin smiled as the perfect place popped into her head.

"I just adore this place!" Kathy's lovely gray eyes were wide with excitement. "I love Mexican food!" She dug her fork into the spicy mixture of refried beans, corn tortilla, melted cheese, and salsa that was on the plate in front of her.

"I'm glad," Caitlin answered. "I remembered how much I liked Mexican food when I was your age. Oh, and I still do," she added quickly, suddenly worried that Kathy would think she was trying to act old.

Another thought occurred to Caitlin as she looked across the table at the pretty young girl. She realized how very much she resembled her brother, Julian. They both had the same gray eyes, although Kathy's weren't steely cold. Kathy was also developing Julian's classic features: his high cheekbones and aquiline nose. It had been more than a year since she had last seen her, and what a difference! Julian's sister was definitely going to be a beauty. Yet, at the moment, Kathy was like a Thoroughbred yearling—she hadn't quite gotten her legs under her.

"I wish there was a Mexican place in Rock Ridge," Kathy said. She made a frown. "We don't even have a McDonald's. There's just the Ridge Cafe. Yuck! I'll be so glad when I can finally get out of Rock Ridge and go to college like Julian did."

At the mention of Julian's name, Caitlin shivered. But she didn't let her uneasiness show. "I think I can understand why you would," she replied softly.

"Julian is so lucky," Kathy rambled on with a happy shrug of her shoulders. "Being a doctor and all." She looked directly at Caitlin. "Did you know he's a real doctor now? I mean, well, he's what they call a resident. But he can perform operations and everything." She sighed. "Gosh, I hope someday I can be something great like that."

"Do you want to be a doctor?" Caitlin asked kindly.

"Oh, no," Kathy said, shaking her head. Her dark hair shimmered as it slid over her shoulders. "I think what I'd really like," she said shyly, "is to be like you. Oh, I know I could never be the president of a company or anything like that. But I really think I'd like to be a businesswoman. I'm good at math, and I know that's important. At least, my teacher says so."

"That's great," Caitlin said with real enthusiasm. "To tell the truth, I wasn't sure what I wanted to do with my life until after I was in college." To be honest, she thought wryly, perhaps she still wasn't sure. "You could even take business courses in high school." Right then she realized that she was going to make sure Kathy Stokes went to college, no matter what. "I think you have a wonderful future ahead of you."

"Oh, I hope so," Kathy said fervently. Then she changed the subject back to her brother. "You know what? Julian's in love." Caitlin paled nervously. Kathy who had never really known what had happened between Julian and Caitlin, just that they'd dated, took Caitlin's response the wrong way. "Oh, how stupid I am. I'm so sorry—I forgot about you and Julian—"

"It's okay. Really—" Caitlin replied, managing a smile. "I was just surprised, that's all."

Kathy eyed her uncertainly, then went on. "Well, she's this great girl he met in Boston. Her name is Ginny. I forgot her last name, but Ginny's a pretty name, huh?" Kathy smiled at her happiness for her brother. "She works for this big investment firm, during the summer. The rest of the year she goes to Harvard. I saw a picture of her, and she is so pretty, really sophisticated and all."

*Ginny!* Ginny Brookes and Julian. It couldn't be, Caitlin told herself as the shock washed over her. But she knew instinctively that it was true. That would explain why Ginny was being so secretive at the engagement party. *She was seeing Julian Stokes.*

Caitlin's thoughts flew back to the time in college when Julian had used not only her roommate, but Ginny as well in his efforts to destroy her. He had hurt Ginny terribly, too. And, in the process, he had almost destroyed the friendship she and Ginny had shared since high school. How could Ginny let herself be taken in by him again? Caitlin had to do something to stop this—this terrible farce of a relationship. If she didn't, Ginny would get hurt again—and this time it would be even more painful.

"Caitlin? Caitlin, did you hear me?"

"I'm sorry," she said, realizing Kathy was speaking to her. "What did you say?"

"Uh," she said and paused bashfully. "I said I hope we could come here again sometime. I really do like this food—and seeing you." She smiled hesitantly. "But maybe I'm—kind of expecting, you know, too much. I mean you're so busy Aunt Caitlin."

"Not at all," Caitlin broke in. "I'll never be too busy to spend time with you. I know I've been away in New York, and I'll be going back there again, probably soon. But I promise you, we're going to spend a lot more time together." She reached her hand across and put it softly on Kathy's arm. "Because I really care about you, Kathy. You're like a sister to me."

# 11

"New York? Why are you going to New York?" With a questioning frown, Caitlin paused midstep to turn and look directly at Howard. It was Saturday morning, and he had come to the estate to talk to Caitlin. They were walking through the formal garden. Nearby, the gardener was busy weeding around the delphiniums. "Howard, look, I know you said the instigator in these corporate problems often turns out to be someone the owner would least expect—someone close," she said and shook her head, "but, if you think for a minute that Jed—"

"No, Caitlin." He put his hand on her arm to reassure her. "I don't suspect your fiancé." And he didn't, but only because he had completed a thorough investigation of Jed

Michaels. He found out, of course, that Jed was exactly what he appeared to be—a good man who was completely in love with Caitlin.

With a nod at Howard's words, Caitlin continued to walk down the path. Walking beside her, Howard thought about Melanie. He was ready to grudgingly admit that she was innocent of any wrongdoing as well. At least any that concerned Ryan Mining. But as for her personally, he still didn't approve of her. He hadn't liked her since she had deceived Caitlin at the restaurant that first day they had met. And he didn't know what to make of Laurence Baxter. Why was he using Melanie? Why all the secrecy? She was a lovely young woman, but—

"Howard?" Caitlin asked, touching his arm. "You didn't answer my question. Why are you going to New York? What do you expect to find there?"

"Hmm?" He forced his mind back to the present conversation. "Oh, I think I've got a strong lead. An insider in the market has agreed to talk to me as long as I don't reveal his name."

"I don't understand," Caitlin said, puzzled. "What is being done is so very wrong. Why would anyone who can help want to be so secretive?"

"Not everyone involved in the stock market

is nice," Howard reminded her gently. "And the company this man works for is one of your competitors; he stands to do very well if Ryan Mining should happen to fold. He would be in serious trouble if anyone knew that he spoke to me."

"Oh, I hate this whole mess," Caitlin said. "I'll be so glad when it's all over."

"That should be soon," Howard told her. "At least, if this lead turns out the way I'm hoping it will." He stopped to look at his watch. "I'd better leave if I'm going to catch the two-ten flight from Dulles."

"Then I'll see you at the airport. That's the flight I'm planning to take, too," Caitlin explained. "I'm going up there to spend the rest of the weekend with Jed."

"No," he said, putting a hand on her arm. "I don't want you to leave the estate. I need to have you here, where I can get in touch with you. And where one of us has access to Ryan Mining."

"But you can't really mean that! Look, I'll be with Jed. Why can't I just give you his number?"

"I'm sorry, I wouldn't ask you if I didn't feel that it was necessary. I may not need to contact you at all. Then again, I might want you to run out to the office to check something for me." His blue eyes looked directly into hers. "Promise you won't leave."

"Oh, all right, I promise," she answered. It meant she would have to call Jed and tell him she was going to have to disappoint him once again. She dreaded making the call. There was one bright spot, though. She could also tell him that Howard had said they were close to finding the culprit, which meant that soon they could get on with their lives.

But hanging up the phone after speaking to Caitlin, Jed wasn't thinking such positive thoughts. To him, as he walked to the window of his apartment and stared down at the wide, quiet surface of the Hudson River below, Caitlin's last-minute cancellation was one more example of how deeply she was involved with her life in Virginia. He was coming in a distant second. It was a situation that he wasn't at all happy with, but he also felt helpless to do anything to change it.

Back at Ryan Acres, Caitlin sat looking at the now quiet phone, a knot in her stomach, she knew she had hurt Jed, but she had had no choice. *Oh, this just has to be over soon*, she hoped fervently. *Jed, Jed—I love you so. Please, just be patient a little while longer. Just a little while.*

In addition to her problems with Jed, Caitlin was also concerned about Ginny. She couldn't believe what she had learned at lunch the day before from Kathy Stokes—that Ginny and Julian were dating. What Caitlin really needed to do was to find an excuse to see her friend, to speak with Ginny face to face. A phone call simply wouldn't do, phone calls could be so cold, impersonal. But what sort of excuse could she dream up that would seem believable to Ginny?

She stood up and began pacing slowly around the library. Coming to the french doors, she leaned against the frame and looked idly out at the lovely, sweeping emerald lawn, bordered by pink, blue, and yellow flowers. The azure water of the pool lay beyond the gardens, and the gabled roof of the stable was beyond that—the stable!

In a burst of inspiration, she spun around and went back to the desk where she had left her briefcase the evening before. Opening it, she took out the horse sale catalog that she received on Thursday. She checked the dates. Yes, the sale was set for the following Saturday. "Perfect—just perfect!" she cried out loud into the empty room. Considering Ginny's long love affair with horses, Caitlin now had a very good reason to invite her old pal down for the weekend.

Picking up the phone, Caitlin's mind was already racing ahead to what she would say. She'd explain that she was thinking of buying some new horses for the Ryan Acres stable—perhaps a new brood mare—or that colt on page thirty-nine.

"Hi Ginny," she said when her old roommate answered the phone. "It's Caitlin—"

Knowing she would have to stay close to the phone in case Howard should need to speak to her, Caitlin nevertheless decided she could not sit in the house waiting for it to ring. Having just gotten off the phone with Ginny, she decided to spend the rest of the day down at the stable. There was a phone there, and should the call come through, one of the stable hands would come to find her.

There was so much to do, she thought as she started upstairs to change into her riding clothes. Duster could be worked out in the ring. And she really hadn't jumped him much lately. She could have the jumps set up. And she would groom him herself. Oh, how she had missed the simple satisfying act of running a brush over a horse's shining coat, smelling the wonderful smells of hay and sawdust bedding and saddle-soaped leather. She smiled to herself happily.

Caitlin paused at the top of the graceful curving staircase, one slim hand on the banister. Maybe she really would buy a horse, but just one. It would be nice to build the stable back up to the size it had been before her grandmother had become ill. Ryan Acres had even been called the best Thoroughbred breeding farm in Virginia once.

Why not, she told herself, entering her bedroom and pulling a pair of breeches and boots from the closet. She kicked off her sandals and slipped out of her slacks. New York was wonderful, but there would always be a Ryan Acres. *Always*, she repeated firmly in her mind.


On Sunday Caitlin had invited Emily and Jim to brunch, and the three of them spent a lovely day together. Now they were standing at the front door saying goodbye.

"Promise you'll come to our house soon," Emily was saying. "I'm dying to show you how we changed that old pantry into a sun porch. It's just perfect. So bright and airy."

At the sound of the phone ringing in the hallway, Emily paused. They all waited while Margaret answered, then announced that it was for Caitlin. "It's Mr. Josso."

"Oh, yes, I do want to take that. Thank you,

Margaret," Caitlin said. "Please tell him I'll be right there." She turned back to her friends.

"We understand," Jim assured her. "We'll just be going." He gave her a friendly smile. "Thanks again for brunch. And please come to our place soon. Bring Jed, too."

"Yes, do. I mean it," Emily added quickly. Then they waved goodbye as Caitlin hurried to answer the phone.

"I'm getting close," Howard's strong, cultured voice said over the line when Caitlin answered the phone. "I've got it narrowed down to three people. I'd like to talk to you about which one you think I should pursue first. All three are in different cities, and since time is of the essence, I think we should go with the person you feel is the most likely culprit."

"Okay. Who are these people?" Caitlin asked breathlessly. Her heart jumped to the back of her throat as she waited for Howard's answer.

"Well, one is a man named Jonathan Worth. I don't think you know him. I don't know how he'd have gotten any dirt on you, but he's a well-known shark when it comes to this style of takeover." He paused to clear his throat slightly. "The other two you know fairly well. One is Marsha Turner—"

"Marsha Turner!" Caitlin cried, aghast. "Her

father was one of my grandmother's oldest friends. Malcom Turner, he's the head of Underwood Mining. Why do you think she has anything to do with the rumors?"

"It could be a case of plain old jealously," Howard explained. "It seems she's been jealous of you for some time. You're both the same age, and you both come from well-to-do families. But while you've made something of yourself, she hasn't. Apparently she dropped out of college in her junior year to bum around Europe. She met some pretty shady characters there, and was even mixed up in drugs for a while."

"How awful," Caitlin whispered, truly sorry.

"Anyway, when her father heard about it, he disinherited her, told her she was on her own from then on. My sources say he thought you were someone she should try to emulate." He paused. "I'm sorry, Caitlin, but she really seems to hate you. So, she has the motive, and she has the contacts through her father."

"All right," Caitlin said. "Who is the third person?"

"Colin Wollman."

"Colin!" she gasped. As soon as she heard the name, all of the horrible things Colin Wollman did to her in the past flooded into her mind. She nodded—it had to be him. *No wait,* she insisted to herself. *Don't be irrational, Caitlin.* Just because she hated the man was no reason to jump to the conclusion that he was guilty. It could be either of the other two. But Howard had said he needed her to pick one person to follow up on first. Her voice firm and resolute, she said, "Investigate Colin first."

"Right. Wollman it is!" Howard replied. "All right, then, I'm off to Washington D.C. That's where he's living now." Howard's voice was encouraging. "You know, Wollman was my first choice, too, but I wanted to get your reaction. I'll give you a call as soon as I have more to report. Or I might see you in person. Whichever way, I promise it won't be long before you have good news."

Dressed in a flowered print sun dress, Caitlin drove the Mercedes to Washington the following Saturday morning. Once again Jed could not get away to join her. Caitlin was meeting Ginny at Dulles Airport. The plane from Boston was on time, and they were soon headed back out into the Virginia countryside toward Warrenton, where the horse sale was being held.

When they arrived, the beginning of the auction was still more than an hour away, but already the parking lot was nearly full. Caitlin had to drive around for what seemed like hours before she found a spot where they could leave the Mercedes.

"Really, I'm so glad you came down today," Caitlin said, giving Ginny's shoulders a warm squeeze as they walked toward the long barns where the horses were stabled.

"Me, too," Ginny replied with a grin that made her look a little less sophisticated and more like her old self. "What are friends for, if not to help other friends spend money on horses? A horse sale is one of my favorite things in the whole world—next to a horse show, that is."

"I do seem to remember that fact," Caitlin replied with a laugh. Watching Ginny as they walked, she noticed now how carefree and happy her old friend looked. She looked so confident in her chic, calf-length skirt and oversize top, short hair shining in the sun. But was it just the excitement of the day that was making her friend look so great? Caitlin wondered. Or was Julian's manipulating charm responsible for the glow on Ginny's face? She truly hoped not. It would make it even more difficult for her to tell Ginny what was on her mind. But that wouldn't stop her. She fully intended to do whatever she could to save Ginny from making a terrible mistake—the same kind of tragic mistake she herself had nearly made when Julian tried his evil tricks on her. He had talked her into believing he was in love with her, when the whole time he had wanted only to destroy her.

Caitlin frowned. There was a problem, however, that was going to make it difficult for Caitlin to talk with Ginny. It had nearly ruined their friendship. Caitlin remembered the time when the three of them had been in college, and Julian had used Ginny to get to Caitlin. He had convinced Ginny to go to Florida during a Christmas break, saying he wanted to be with her, but also suggesting that Caitlin might like to go along. Then, once they were in Florida, he had dumped Ginny at a dance to take Caitlin for a walk on a moonlit beach. Caitlin had been so overcome by Julian's magnetic charm that she had gone, leaving her friend alone at the dance.

The next morning when she went to find Ginny to apologize for what had happened, Caitlin found that her friend had already flown home. It had been ages before Ginny spoke to her again. Would the same thing happen this time? Would Ginny think she was meddling? Probably. But wasn't Ginny's happiness what really counted?

"What's the matter?" Ginny suddenly asked, breaking into Caitlin's thoughts. "Is something wrong?"

"Hmmmm—what?" Caitlin glanced at Ginny, realizing she had been ignoring her. "Oh, sorry," she said with a little laugh. "I guess I was trying to decide which would be the better buy, a brood mare or that colt I pointed out in the catalog."

"Are you sure that's all?" Ginny persisted, looking at her questioningly. "You looked as though it was something a lot more serious."

"I'm positive, really," Caitlin said with a reassuring smile. They were almost at the main entrance. "Look, why don't I go register with the office, give them my credit information so I can get a number to bid with. You go find us some coffee. I sure could use some." She turned, walking away before Ginny could pursue the subject further.

Ten minutes later, Styrofoam cups of steaming coffee in their hands, they strolled along one of the barn aisles.

Ginny paused to look into a stall. "Hey, Caitlin, come here and check out this little sorrel filly."

"Hmmm—nice," Caitlin agreed, looking at the horse. "But I don't remember seeing her in the catalog." Checking the number on the stall, she flipped through the pages. "Oh, yes, here she is," Caitlin said, showing Ginny the photograph and description. "She looks a lot different up close. That's a bad photo." She studied the filly. "But I think you pegged it when you said *little*. She's a bit too short for my taste."

"She'd make a lovely lightweight hunter. She has good shoulders with a nice slope to them. She'd be a nice comfortable ride."

Caitlin nodded. "Let's go on. I still want to see that colt before the bidding begins."

Several buyers were standing near the colt's stall when they found it. From their remarks, it was obvious that there would be some spirited bidding when it came time for the young horse to come up to the block. They walked away and Ginny and Caitlin moved up to the stall door to see for themselves.

Neither girl said a word for a few minutes as they checked out the shining chestnut coat of the horse that was looking back at them with intelligent eyes. Ginny was the first to speak.

"Oh, wow, Caitlin. He's absolutely gorgeous." She shook her head in admiration. "Makes me wish I was still living down here. I think I'd bid on him myself."

"Really?" Caitlin said thoughtfully, still admiring the horse.

"You'd better believe it."

"I don't know," Caitlin said, folding the catalog back to the description of the colt. "His bloodlines really are pretty impressive, but they're straight racing lines. Look!" She pointed to the diagram of the horse's background.

"Wow! Bold Ruler," Ginny said, impressed. "I should have guessed from his conformation."

"Well, that could make him too hyper to be a good hunter."

"Maybe. But it could also make him fast. You'd probably have to hold him back to keep him from passing the master of the hunt," Ginny commented lightly and smiled.

"Which wouldn't be in the best of taste," Caitlin said back wryly.

"So why don't you race him?" Ginny said with a sparkle in her eyes. "Did you ever think of doing that?"

"Would I ever love to do something like that. But that's entirely different, and you know it. A full-time trainer, licenses, jockey, manager—that's serious business. And I can just imagine what Jed would say." She shook her head. Silently she was wondering how he would react if she actually did end up buying one or two horses. Probably just fine, she told herself confidently. After all, hadn't Jed grown up on a ranch? And didn't he love horses as much as she did? Of course he did. She knew he'd be just as excited as she was if she bought a horse like the one she was now admiring. But racing? No, she guessed not. Owning horses and being a New York attorney didn't really sound as though they would make a good mix.

"So?" prompted Ginny. "Are you going to bid on him or not?"

"I don't know," Caitlin admitted hesitantly. "I do like him a lot. But I'm also pretty sure that with those bloodlines, he's going to end up being fairly pricey."

"Maybe, maybe not. But there's only one way to find out." With a grin, she linked her arm through Caitlin's. "And that's to go to the auction building so we can get a good seat. Just have your checkbook ready. Because I have a definite feeling that"—she checked the name in the catalog—"Rule My Heart is going to end up in the Ryan Acres stable."

As Caitlin thought, the bidding was fierce. But by the time the gavel came down for the last time, the chestnut colt belonged to Caitlin. So did the little golden red filly they had seen earlier. It was the filly's spirit in the ring that had convinced Caitlin to buy her. She was extremely happy about both her purchases as she arranged for the two horses to be delivered to the estate the following Saturday.

Her exuberance faded somewhat as she and Ginny drove back toward Ryan Acres. The sun was low in the sky, and shadows stretched across the rolling grassy pasture of the hunt country. Caitlin still hadn't talked to Ginny. She had decided during the afternoon to wait until they were back at the estate, perhaps while they were having a glass of wine before dinner.

"Thanks for inviting me to stay the night," Ginny said, breaking what had been an extended silence. "I hope that includes a swim tomorrow morning and a nice leisurely breakfast on the terrace. I don't know anyone in Boston with a pool, so if I ever want to go swimming, I have to do it at this club I belong to. Indoor pools just aren't the same."

"Absolutely!" Caitlin assured her friend with a smile. "I'll even have Mrs. Crowley whip up some of those blueberry scones you love so much."

"Fantastic!" Ginny exclaimed, stretching her arms out in front of her, then leaning back against the comfortable leather seat. "And tonight, we can stay up all night talking. It'll be just like old times." She sighed contentedly. "Right, Caitlin?"

# 12

Arriving back at the estate, Caitlin asked Rollins to ask Mrs. Crowley to serve dinner in the rear sitting room at about eight-thirty.

"Is that okay with you?" she asked, turning to look at Ginny after glancing at her watch. "That'll give us time to shower and change, and then relax with a glass of wine before we eat."

"Sounds good to me." Ginny agreed with a nod.

Half an hour later, showered and wearing a comfortable jumpsuit, her dark hair tied back with a colorful scarf, Caitlin went downstairs. She spoke briefly to Rollins, asking him to bring a bottle of chilled white wine, along with a plate of Brie and some crackers, into the rear sitting room. Then she went there herself. Ginny was still upstairs.

She glanced around the room, which had always been one of her favorite places in the house. It opened onto the glass-enclosed conservatory, which was filled with tropical plants and the flowering lavender and white orchids that Barnes, the gardener, tended so lovingly. The outside doors were open and a cool evening breeze drifted softly in, bringing with it the fragrances of the late-summer flowers. Yes, she told herself, the room was a good place for her talk with Ginny. It was a comfortable room, done in greens and pale golds, not like the more formal living room or the somewhat stuffy library.

The small table had already been set for two. Caitlin walked over and straightened a fork slightly. Her heart was already beginning to pound. God, how she hated having to say what was on her mind. She hoped she could be diplomatic enough to convince Ginny she was making a mistake with Julian, but not hurt her feelings. Maybe, she thought with a glimmer of bright hope, maybe she should just leave the whole thing alone, just let it work itself out. And it would eventually, wouldn't it? But, no, that wasn't fair. What if he really hurt Ginny this time? The bottom line was her friend's happiness, and there was nothing Caitlin could do but go ahead with her plan.

"That's a pretty jumpsuit," Ginny said, her voice surprising Caitlin. She hadn't heard her friend come into the room.

"Oh, thanks," she said, turning to smile at Ginny. "I found it at Saks earlier this summer. I do have to admit that one of the nice things about living in New York is the shopping." On the edge of babbling nervously, she forced herself to calm down. "I love that skirt you're wearing." Ginny's skirt was ankle length, full, and made of wildly printed tropical cotton. With it she wore a sleeveless cotton knit top. "It's not very Boston, though."

"No, it's not," Ginny agreed, crossing the room to sit on one of the comfortable sofas. "I got it in St. Martin. We flew down there for a long weekend last . . ." Just then she stopped speaking, her words trailing off. She glanced down at the skirt and picked lightly at a loose thread. When she looked back up, she said, "I never can get over those orchids. They're so gorgeous."

At that moment Rollins came into the room with their wine and the cheese and crackers. No one spoke while he set the tray down, poured the wine into two glasses, and left.

Caitlin watched as Ginny sipped her drink. She moved to a chair across from her friend and sat down. *Come on, Caitlin*, she told herself, *this is Ginny, your oldest and dearest friend. Get on with it*.

"Hi, you two!" a bright, breathless voice called from the hall. It was Melanie, arms filled with bags and packages. Caitlin remembered she had said something about going shopping for some new clothes. Obviously she had found what she wanted. Her face was beaming with happiness. "I just have a second—I'm already late. I've got to get ready for my date with Laurence." She shifted her packages to her other arm. "But first I wanted to find out how you did at the sale. Did you buy a horse?"

"Two," Ginny spoke for Caitlin.

"Really? Hey, that's super." She nodded, her reply sounding as though she had just heard Caitlin had bought a couple of new records instead of two horses, valued at one hundred and twenty thousand dollars. "Well, I really have to run." Trying to wave around all her packages, she breezed out again.

As soon as she was out of earshot, Ginny glanced over at Caitlin. She raised one eyebrow slightly. "Laurence? Did she mean Laurence Baxter?"

"Yes," Caitlin replied, sighing out loud.

"Somehow I don't think of Laurence Baxter as Melanie's type. I mean, I know you dated him in high school and all that. He was so nice then. But when I talked to him at your engagement party, I got the distinct feeling that he had changed. It's as though he's a weaker, disillusioned person or something. I don't know—"

"I think you're very right. I don't know what's happened to him in the last few years, but he definitely isn't the same person we knew in high school. You know, he's also seeing Nancy Robinson, and even if he weren't, I definitely agree that he's wrong for Melanie." She paused. Here was the perfect opening to mention Julian. "Uh, Ginny, I've been meaning to talk to you about something—about Julian, actually."

"Julian!" Ginny cried in surprise, her face becoming a mask of stone.

"Yes, Julian," Caitlin repeated. Setting her glass down on the coffee table between them, she looked her friend straight in the eyes. "I know that you're dating him. Oh, I found out by accident," she hastened to add. "I was having lunch with Kathy, and she just happened to mention—"

"So—" Ginny responded calmly.

"You're my best friend, Ginny. And I hate it that you felt you had to hide your relationship with Julian from me."

"And just what would you have done if I had come to you and said that Julian and I are in love?" Ginny's voice was harshly cynical. "You wouldn't have jumped up and down with joy."

An unhappy frown marred Caitlin's forehead. "No," she admitted. "To be perfectly honest, I guess I would have done exactly what I'm going to try to do now, and that's talk some sense into you." As soon as the words were out of her mouth, she was sorry she had sounded so superior. She saw Ginny's eyes narrowing. "I don't want to hurt you, but I can't help the feelings I have about Julian Stokes." She leaned forward. "Ginny, how could you forgive him for what he did to you in Florida? How could you forget how much he hurt you? I don't want to see that happen again."

Ginny closed her eyes momentarily, then opened them again. The look in them was cold, distant. "This is why you invited me down here this weekend, isn't it? You didn't want my advice on buying horses, did you? You just felt you had to straighten out poor, stupid Ginny again, right?" She shook her head and stood up. Pushing past Caitlin, she walked to the table. She swung back around and cried, "If you hadn't gotten to the subject over wine, would you have sat there pitying me as we talked? Would you have kept wondering how I could be so dumb?"

"Ginny!" Caitlin pleaded. Getting quickly to her feet, she started toward her friend.

"No!" Ginny raised a hand to stop Caitlin. "You just can't give me any credit at all, can you, Caitlin? I'm an adult just like you, and I'm capable of making my own decisions without your help. Especially when it's so obvious that you'll always hate Julian no matter what. If I said he had changed, you'd probably never believe it."

"Changed? Julian?"

"See!" Ginny accused. "But he has changed. A few minutes ago we were talking about how Laurence changed—well, Julian has, too. Only not for the worse, but for the better."

"Ginny, no, you're wrong. He's just using his charm again—that evil, manipulating charm of his. He'll only hurt you. I know he will!"

"No, you *don't* know!" Ginny shot back, gripping the edge of the table with one hand. "And speaking of changing, it's a pretty safe bet that you'll never change. You'll never learn that you're no longer the most popular girl in school. You can't change people's lives with a whisper in someone's ear now."

"What?" Caitlin's eyes flew open in surprise. "Is that what you think I'm doing?"

"Aren't you?" Ginny replied. "You still think you make the rules, don't you? Well, not for me—and not for Julian. He loves me, and as long as he does, I'll stay with him."

"Ginny! Ginny," Caitlin said with sad determination. "Can't you see? That's simply one more example of how conniving Julian can be. He's turned you against me. Please," she pleaded, "you must believe me."

"What I believe, Caitlin," Ginny said, her voice even and cool, "is that I no longer wish to count you as one of my friends. I made a mistake when I forgave you that first time you walked off with Julian." She took a deep breath, letting it out slowly. "I won't make that mistake again, you can count on it. Now I'm going to go upstairs and pack. If you'd have Rollins call me a cab, I'd appreciate it." Then she swept past Caitlin and out into the hall.

"Oh, damn," Caitlin said softly as she sank into the nearest chair. After a moment she rang for Rollins. When the butler appeared, she said, "I'm afraid Miss Brookes will be leaving shortly to go to the airport. Will you please bring the Bentley around and then carry her luggage down." She glanced at the table, all set for dinner. Letting out an angry sigh, she added, "And I would appreciate it if you would tell Mrs. Crowley that there won't be any need to serve dinner."

After Rollins left, Caitlin stared across the room at the empty sofa where Ginny had been sitting. Could they ever, she wondered, be friends again? At the moment, it didn't seem possible. And it was all because of Julian Stokes.

About an hour later the phone rang. Caitlin, hoping it was Ginny calling to say she wanted to come back and talk things out, picked up the phone without waiting for the maid to answer.

But instead of Ginny, it was Howard. "Hi, Caitlin. Look, I'm on my way back from Washington—I'm on the car phone—and I'm not far from Ryan Acres. I've got some news for you, and I'd like to come over and discuss it, if that's all right?"

"Of course," Caitlin said.

Ten minutes later the maid opened the door for Howard. Caitlin was standing right behind her, waiting to welcome him.

At the same time Melanie was on her way down the curving staircase. She was dressed for her date with Laurence in dark green linen pants and a green and blue beaded top, which looked absolutely lovely with her skin and the warm brown of her hair that curled softly around her pretty face. Seeing Howard, she stopped short. The happy expression on her face changed to a more guarded look.

Caitlin, seeing Melanie's reaction, was somewhat puzzled, and she glanced from Jed's sister back toward Howard. For just a moment she caught the briefest glimpse of a look on his face she could only term as disapproval. Then the look was gone. He acknowledged Melanie's presence with a polite nod before turning to Caitlin with a glad smile. "The news I have for you is good, Caitlin. But I'd like to speak to you in private."

"Yes, of course," she answered, glancing once more in Melanie's direction. But Melanie, her head held high, was already at the bottom of the stairs. Without looking at Caitlin, she called out easily, "I'm going now. Don't wait up. I don't know how late I'll be." She stepped out the door and closed it behind her.

While not completely dismissing what had just occurred, Caitlin reminded herself that perhaps she was overreacting. Maybe she was reading something into it that wasn't really there. After all, she was still upset over Ginny's departure.

"Is the library all right?" she asked, glancing up at Howard's handsome face.

"Fine," he replied, following her. With the doors closed behind them, Caitlin turned and asked automatically, "Would you like some coffee? Or perhaps something to drink?"

"No, thank you," he replied. Taking her

159

hands in his, he said without preamble, "It was Colin Wollman, Caitlin."

Caitlin felt a rush of relief pass through her. "Are you sure?" she whispered. Her voice was so soft that if Howard hadn't been standing immediately in front of her, he wouldn't have heard her.

"Yes," he assured her. "And by now, he knows you are being informed. It's over, Caitlin. He shouldn't bother you anymore."

"Thank goodness," she replied with a thoughtful nod. Quietly breaking her hands free from his, she walked across the length of the room to stand in front of the fireplace. Her grandmother's portrait hung just above where she stood. Silently she gazed up at the regal face of the woman who had ruled Ryan Mining, and her childhood, with uncompromising resoluteness.

Howard noticed the strong resemblance between grandmother and granddaughter. Not so much in looks—although they were both beautiful, but in different ways—but in their resolve. Yes, Caitlin Ryan was definitely a woman of character, someone other women would want to emulate. And he knew then that he would admire her forever.

Caitlin turned back to face Howard, her face confident. "I suppose what we should do now is let people know who was responsible for the rumors. Oh, I know it needn't be too obvious—not like a press conference." She tipped her head to one side, thinking. "Do you suppose it's possible to leak this information to the press so that it doesn't appear as though we're giving out a press release?"

"It's very possible. In fact, it's done all the time. It's just that the average person isn't aware of it."

"Good!" She crossed the room again. "Then I think I'll get started on that right away. I'll see if I can get hold of Randolph and ask him to drop by first thing in the morning. He's the first one I want to talk to." *And after that, I'll call Jed,* she thought with a smile.

"Well, it looks as though you have matters under control," he said. "So I think I'll leave."

"Please, Howard, don't rush off," she said. "Not after you've brought me such great news. Do stay and have a drink now."

"Thanks, but I really must go," he replied. "It's been a long week, and I think I'd just like to go home."

"Of course. I understand." She walked him to the door. Rising on her toes, she put her hands on his shoulders and gently kissed his cheek. "Thank you again," she said softly.

"You're welcome," he replied before slipping out the door and into the night.

# 13

By Thursday the *Wall Street Journal*, the Washington *Post*, *The New York Times*, and the Los Angeles *Times* had run stories about Colin's rumor-spreading campaign, calling it an aborted takeover attempt. The decision had been made jointly by Caitlin and Randolph Woods, as well as two other members of the board, that it would be wiser to let the public believe it was a takeover attempt, and not an act of revenge. As long as the thrust of the story was that it was a takeover attempt, it was just another story in the day-to-day world of business. If word of a revenge plot got out, every cheap rag of a paper would have jumped on the story. Caitlin's face would have been seen on the front pages of grocery store tabloids across the country. She certainly didn't want that for herself, or for Ryan Mining.

It was true that Colin Wollman would not actually be going to jail. But she felt he was nevertheless being punished. No one would want to involve himself in any business dealings with Colin for a long time to come.

Later, sitting at her desk, copies of the national papers spread in front of her, Caitlin felt happier than she had in weeks. The fear and uncertainty that Colin had caused was over. He wouldn't be coming into her life again. Her projects with the company were definitely shaping up, too. And she had a new, loyal friend in Howard Josso.

Caitlin was even hopeful that her fight with Ginny was over. She reached for the letter that had been sent overnight mail, scanning her friend's slanted writing once again. No, she was certain she hadn't misinterpreted Ginny's words. She had written in answer to the letter Caitlin had sent Express Mail on Monday. In it, Caitlin had told Ginny how terrible she felt about hurting her, explaining that she couldn't help feeling the way she did because of her own experience with Julian. But she also admitted that people did change, and maybe she had been too hard on Julian. She added that if she was willing to admit as much, she hoped that Ginny would at least rethink some of the things she had said. Caitlin wanted very much to save their friendship.

She looked back down at Ginny's letter:

> I'm sorry you disapprove of my relationship with Julian, but you're wrong—he has changed. And I love him. If you can accept that, I'm sure we can stay friends. Let's try at least.
> Your old friend,
> Ginny

Well, it was a beginning, anyway, she told herself. Their friendship would survive—it always had.


Colin Wollman was sitting in a booth in one of the seediest bars he had ever seen. He had already tossed back two shots of scotch, and was now nursing a scotch and water. There was an angry scowl on his face as he looked at the expensive gold watch on his wrist. It was late. Where was that low-life, anyway? he wondered. When he made the appointment with Eddie, he expected him, at least, to show up on time, especially considering how much money was at stake.

Thinking about the money, Colin became nervous. Trying to appear unobtrusive, he felt the packet in his inside jacket pocket, just to be sure it was still there. It was enough to keep Eddie happy for a long time—enough to take him out of the country if that was what he wanted. But Colin was fairly sure he wouldn't go, at least not until he had finished the job and collected the rest of the money. Colin finished his drink and asked the cocktail waitress to bring him another.

The woman brought it to him and he paid her from a pile of bills lying on the tabletop. She left, and he stared at his drink. So Caitlin Ryan thought she had had the final say, did she? Well, just wait until she got the surprise he had planned for her.

But it wouldn't happen unless that creep, Eddie, showed up and got his instructions. Colin looked at the door and frowned, and just as he did, Eddie walked in.

Eddie was a short, wiry man, about forty years old. He was standing just inside the bar, looking around. Colin waited, and finally the man noticed him and came toward the booth. With an amused smile, Eddie slid into the seat opposite Colin.

"It's about time," Colin grumbled. "What kept you, anyway?"

"Nervous?" Eddie asked, slouching back against the wooden seat. "It's none of your business, but it you must know, I was with the police."

"The police!" Colin's voice shot up a decibel.

"Calm yourself, buddy," Eddie sneered. "It was about another matter. Nothing to do with you."

"Did they follow you here?"

"Of course not. What do you take me for?" Eddie scratched his chin with a ragged thumbnail. "I know my business. I wouldn't be considered one of the best on the East Coast if I didn't." He leaned forward, placing his elbows on the table. "Did you bring the money?"

"Yes. Half of it—just as we agreed." Colin started to reach into his pocket.

"Whoa! Don't be so obvious, mate," Eddie stopped him. "Someone could be watching. Wait till I tell you it's okay." Colin nodded. "Now," Eddie said in a low voice. "What do you want me to torch?"

"A barn."

"A barn?" Eddie shook his head. "You're going to give me five grand to burn down a stupid barn?"

"Okay, it's a stable," Colin said, his voice as low as Eddie's. "It's on a large estate about seventy miles from here in Virginia. Here are the directions to the estate. The barn is filled with very expensive Thoroughbred horses."

"Ah! A horse barn. I'm very good at them. I've done a couple of racetracks," he said, nodding knowledgeably. "Lots of insurance money on them nags. Are they yours?"

"This has nothing to do with insurance money," Colin snapped impatiently.

"Whatever." Eddie shrugged. "You do want me to make it look accidental, though, don't you?"

Colin frowned. He hadn't thought about

whether it should look like an accident—a fire was a fire. All he cared about was that Caitlin would stand there helplessly as her precious horses burned. She'd hear them scream and thrash around in their stalls, unable to save them. It was the most hurtful act he could think of, one that would give him great pleasure to read about in the papers. It would be even better if Caitlin knew he was responsible for causing the tragedy. Yes, very satisfying. But it could also land him in jail. He looked at Eddie. "Right. I want it to look accidental. Definitely."

"You got it. Now is there a special time you want me to do this, or can I torch the place when I want? I like it much better if I can decide for myself. That way I can case the place and pick a time when no one'll be around."

The arsonist grinned at Colin. "Night's best. That way you can be at a party or a restaurant, someplace where you'll be seen and remembered by lots of people."

"How about this weekend?"

"Hmmm. Today's Thursday," Eddie said, thinking for a moment. "I can go out there and look it over now, I guess. Yeah, I think I can pencil the job into my social calendar." He laughed at his own imitation of a busy executive.

Colin wasn't amused. "How do you plan to do it?"

"You mean torch the place?" Eddie shook his head. "That's my business, you don't got to worry about that. That's what you're paying me for," he said eyeing the slight bulge in the front of Colin's tailored suit jacket. "Speaking of money"—his eyes slid sideways toward the bar, then back to Colin—"you can pass that bundle over now."

Eddie quickly pocketed the money Colin handed him. As he slid from the booth, he gave Colin a warning. "Just remember, this is only half of what you owe me for this job. I'll expect the other half as soon as the job's completed."

"Don't worry, you'll get it," Colin promised.

"You'd better make sure of that, buddy." Eddie touched the front of his cap in a mocking salute. "You wouldn't want word to get around that a certain fellow was supposed to pay me and didn't, now would you?"

As Eddie left the bar, Colin felt an urge to get up and wash his hands. He hated dealing with scum like that.

He started to leave right away, then thought better of it. Perhaps he should wait a bit before going. He didn't want to take the chance of being linked to anything Eddie was involved in. Settling back into the booth, he signaled for the waitress.

"Another scotch," he ordered. "And this time see to it that the glass is clean."

# 14

"Oh, Jed, the colt and filly just got here. They're both as gorgeous as they were last weekend when I saw them at the sale," Caitlin said, her enthusiasm bubbling over. "You're going to love Rule My Heart. I've given him a nickname, though. He looks so sure of himself, so confident, that I've decided to call him King. And the filly—Jed, she's just the sweetest thing. I love her name, too. It fits her. Remember I told you she's a sorrel, and her coat is like blazing fire? It's golden red—"

"So what's her name?" Jed asked, sounding resigned.

"Autumn Sunshine. But I'm just going to call her Sunshine. Oh, I wish you'd been here when they arrived."

"I thought I explained when we talked

yesterday that I couldn't come down. I've got a lot of work to do," Jed said, sounding irritated. "I can't just drop everything to come down and look at a couple of horses. I mean, you have your hobby, and I think that's great. I'm really very happy for you," he went on. "But I've got work to do."

"But it's Saturday, Jed," Caitlin said, her voice now subdued.

"I'm an attorney, Caitlin. My job is hardly nine to five. You could have come here, you know."

"I had to be *here* for the horses, you know that. But, Jed, other attorneys find free time—like Howard," Caitlin said. "He finds time to relax. In fact, he's coming over in a few minutes to play tennis."

"Great!" Jed's harsh voice shot through the line, making the word sound like a curse. "When did you invite him over? As soon as you found I wouldn't be coming?"

"As a matter of fact, yes," Caitlin answered coolly. "Jed, really, he's a friend. He'd done a lot for Ryan Mining. He's virtually saved it single-handedly."

"And I've done nothing to help you, is that it?" Jed snapped. This was a sore point with him. He honestly would have liked to help Caitlin through the trouble with Colin, but he had had so much work of his own to do. A law associate's life wasn't easy. Besides that, he didn't know the law that would have been of help to Caitlin. Still . . .

"Jed?"

"Look, I really do have a lot of work piled up here. I'd better hang up and get to it. I'll give you a call this evening," he said brusquely. "We can talk more then. That is, if you're not too tired from your tennis game. Or, if you haven't gone out to dinner with your beloved Howard."

"Jed!"

"So long, Caitlin."

Jed slammed the phone down so hard it bounced in the cradle. He stared at it, astonished. What had come over him? he asked himself. Where had the conversation gone wrong? He thought back over it.

Well, for one thing, he had lied, and he was feeling guilty about that. He stared at the desk in front of him. It was his father's old desk, the one he had brought from the ranch when he first moved to New York. The top of it, except for the phone and a double silver frame with two photos of Caitlin, was clear. Sure, he had brought a couple of briefs home to work on. But he could have easily taken time off to fly down to Ryan Acres. If he had wanted to, he could have been with Caitlin when those blasted horses arrived.

But *horses* were part of the problem. Everything Caitlin was doing reinforced one thing: Caitlin was staying in Virginia. That weekend, he had decided to take a stand, to dig in his heels and make her come up to New York. He wanted her to realize New York was where her home was now—not that estate in Virginia where she had grown up.

He softly moaned, putting his head in his hands. "I'm so afraid of losing her," he whispered.

Well, this was certainly a great way to do it, he told himself sternly, forcing himself to straighten up. He looked at the two photographs of Caitlin—one a close-up of her beautiful face, the other a full-length shot of her with her horse, Duster. In the latter, the photographer had caught her laughing happily while stroking Duster's majestic head.

He had to admit it, Caitlin and horses went hand in hand. Maybe he should consider a compromise and not be so hardheaded about how much time they spent in New York, or in Virginia. Maybe he should even go down there that very afternoon. Hell, why not? It wasn't all that late. He could catch the shuttle, and tell her he had cleared up his work quickly. No, that was wrong. He would tell her that he had come to his senses, that she was more important than any work. He stood and smiled for the first time that day. He'd just pack an overnight bag, grab a jacket, and catch a cab to the airport. It was almost four now—he could be there by seven.

Melanie was in her room reading when she heard a soft knock on the door. "Come in," she called out.

The door opened, and Margaret came in. She was holding a box of long-stemmed red roses. "These just came for you, miss."

"Oh!" Melanie exclaimed with happy surprise. "How lovely. I adore red roses."

"They are beautiful, aren't they?" Margaret agreed as she set the box down on the low table beside the chaise where Melanie sat.

Melanie could hardly wait until the maid closed the door behind her to read the small white card.

Mel—
I have a wonderful surprise. Meet me at *our* special inn at six this evening.
Love, L

*A surprise!* Laurence said he had a surprise. Melanie felt like laughing and jumping up and down. It could only mean one thing—that he had finally told Nancy they were through. She smiled, feeling warm all over. Why else would he have specified their special place, the Chelsea Creek Inn. Hugging herself, she whirled around the room dizzily. What would she wear? Something very romantic and special. Because that night was going to be special, she was sure of it.

After going back and forth for half an hour, Melanie finally decided what to wear. It was a full, white cotton dress dotted with pink flowers. The dress had tiny shoulder straps, and a matching soft jacket. It was the most romantic outfit she could find in her closet.

As she walked up the flagstone path to the front door of the Chelsea Creek Inn later, the light scent of her favorite perfume surrounding her, she felt truly feminine and lovely.

Laurence was there, waiting in the quiet, shadowy lobby when she arrived. He rose from his chair and came toward her with a smile on his handsome face that sent her pulses racing.

"Hi, Mel." He pulled her into his arms, giving her a quick kiss. Stepping back, but still holding her around the waist, he said, "You look absolutely gorgeous."

"Hmmmm." She looked coyly up at him, her green eyes twinkling. "Do you really mean that?"

"Of course," he answered with a low, husky chuckle. He kissed her again, his mouth lingering against hers a little longer this time. "Oooh," he murmured. "Maybe we'd better not stay here." Turning toward the door, one arm still around her waist, he said, "So, what is this wonderful surprise you've planned?"

"Me?" She pulled away from him and looked at him blankly. "What do you mean me? You're the one with the surprise."

"Me!" He looked confused. "Melanie, I don't know what's going on. Did you or didn't you send me a carnation this afternoon with a note in the box saying that you had a surprise, and that I was to meet you here at six?"

"A carnation?" Melanie looked at him with round, questioning eyes. "No—" She shook her head slowly. "I didn't send you anything." She was absolutely terrified to ask the question in her mind, but she had to. "D-Didn't you send me red roses this afternoon?"

"No—no, I didn't." Laurence looked pale beneath his dark tan.

"Then," Melanie said, her voice was barely a whisper, "who did?"

"*Surprise!* I sent the flowers to both of you." Melanie spun around at the sound of the light, bitter voice. She saw a slender blond girl stepping out from behind the lush foliage of a nearby indoor plant. "So it really was a surprise, wasn't it?" She laughed sharply.

Melanie noticed that the girl was beautiful, with fine, delicate features and shoulder-length, honey-colored hair. She was the type of young woman Melanie had seen at charity balls. At that moment, however, her dark eyes seemed to be impaling Melanie with a dagger-like stare.

"*Nancy!*" Laurence gasped. He dropped his arm from around Melanie's waist and stared at Nancy. "What are you doing here?"

"Catching you, Laurence," Nancy said, walking slowly toward them. "I had sort of hoped you wouldn't show up, that you really didn't care about Melanie." She smiled mirthlessly. "But, you do, don't you."

"Uh, Nancy—" Laurence shot her a sorry smile. "You've got this all wrong. I swear."

"Come on, Laurence, don't lie." Nancy shook her head sadly. "You've been caught and you know it." She turned and looked at Melanie. "So, this is the girl you met at Caitlin Ryan's party. Well, at least you have good taste—she's quite pretty."

Melanie stepped forward. "I'm really sorry, Nancy. We meant to tell you a lot earlier. I told Laurence that it wasn't fair to keep leading you on. But then he said that your mother was so sick, and that you were having a rough enough time as it was." She shrugged helplessly. "Really, we didn't mean to hurt you."

"What are you talking about?" Nancy asked, looking confused. She glanced over at Laurence for an explanation. "What is she talking about?"

"Oh, what a mess," Laurence mumbled.

Now Melanie was beginning to wonder what was going on. Had he lied to her? She grabbed Laurence's arm and turned him toward her. "Nancy's mother *is* sick, isn't she? You were going to tell Nancy about us, weren't you?"

Laurence was silent. Then he swallowed hard and tried to explain. "I'm sorry—"

Melanie looked at Nancy. "Your mother never was sick, was she?"

"No, she hasn't been in the hospital in years."

"Oh, no. I feel so stupid," Melanie whispered. "That line is so old, I can't believe I fell for it."

"I-I'm, uh, sorry. Really I am. You were just so pretty when I saw you at that party. I couldn't resist. I wanted to know you."

"So you lied to me?" Melanie asked. "You let me believe in you when you didn't mean a word of it."

"I wanted to—really I did. Oh, hell! Nancy and I are made for each other. We've known each other a long time—we belong together. I can't leave her. I'm sorry, Melanie," Laurence

177

repeated. "I never wanted anything like this to happen."

"But I want you!" Melanie's voice was suddenly pleading.

"Now you see the difference between us, Laurence," Nancy said.

Melanie stood there, feeling almost paralyzed as she watched them go. As the door finally closed behind them, she sank into the nearest chair. She could feel her knees begin to shake. Her eyes filled, and two tears slid silently down her cheeks.

A desk clerk, who had seen part of the confrontation, came over and asked solicitously if there was anything he could do to help.

"No—no, thank you," Melanie replied with a loud sniff. Getting to her feet, she turned to him and dabbed at her eyes. "I'm going home—and I never, ever want to see this place again!"

"Yes. Yes, ma'am," he said, leaping back a step, absolutely cowed. He continued to stay a safe distance from her as she swept from the lobby, her head held high.

Howard and Caitlin had finished their tennis game and were sitting on the terrace sipping tall, icy glasses of lemonade when Melanie came rushing through the house.

"Caitlin! Caitlin," she cried, running out

onto the terrace. "It was so awful." Then she saw Howard was there and stopped behind a chair, grasping its back for support. A terrible sob rushed from her lips, then she covered her mouth with one hand.

"Melanie!" Caitlin rose quickly and went to Melanie's side. Putting her arm around the girl's shoulders, she asked, "What is it? What's wrong?"

"Oh, Caitlin," Melanie wailed. Then, turning her back on Howard, she poured out her story. Keeping her voice as low as possible, she told Caitlin everything.

Caitlin listened quietly, helping Melanie to sit down, then sitting beside her. She stroked Melanie's shoulder soothingly.

When Melanie was finished, Caitlin searched her pockets for a tissue to give her. But she didn't have one. Howard, who had heard everything, got up from his chair, came over and handed Melanie a clean handkerchief from his pocket. "Here," he said brusquely.

"T-thank you," Melanie whispered.

Caitlin was trying to figure out what to say to Melanie. Although she was pleased that her affair with Laurence had finally come to an end, she also hated to see Melanie hurt. Deciding how to put her words most diplomatically, she opened her mouth to speak. But Howard spoke first.

"I really don't think you have all that much to cry about," he told Melanie coldly. "It seems to me that the person who was really hurt by this deception was Nancy."

"I beg your pardon!" Melanie's head snapped around, and she glared up at Howard. "And just who asked for your opinion?"

"No one, I'm giving you my opinion free. And considering the value of my opinions, that's darn cheap. But I think you need it, so it's yours."

"What if I don't want it?" Melanie shot back, her eyes dark with fury.

"Then don't take it. But, if you're half as smart as I think you are, you will. Forget about Laurence. Consider it a lesson learned. You put your trust in the wrong kind of guy, and next time be honest with everyone." He looked embarrassed by his own vehemence. "Just don't go sneaking around again," he added more softly. "You'll end up hurting yourself and everyone else."

Melanie snapped her head toward Caitlin. "I'm leaving." She stood up. "I don't need this." She marched toward the door, then swung around. "I'm going back to New York tomorrow. There's nothing more for me here." Her gaze narrowing, she glared at Howard. "At least I have friends there."

"Howard!" Caitlin cried, turning on him the

second Melanie was out of earshot. "How could you have been so cold to her? She was positively devastated. I mean, I don't approve of what she's been doing, either, but this is not the time to moralize. Right now she needs compassion and understanding."

"You're too soft on her, Caitlin," Howard told her. "She needs a strong hand."

"But not from you, certainly," Caitlin replied firmly. "Howard, I'm not blind. I've noticed that there's some sort of animosity between the two of you. I'm not asking what it is because it's none of my business, but now is not the time to rub it in."

"Right. You're absolutely right," Howard admitted. "I'm sorry."

"Well, I'm going upstairs to see if there is anything else I can do for her right now."

"And I think I'd better leave."

"Maybe it's best," Caitlin said. Then, softening, she added, "For now, anyway."


Feeling uncomfortable, Howard drove his car away from the estate. Caitlin was very important to him, and he knew he had upset her. He hadn't meant to, but Melanie always got to him somehow.

Howard was so preoccupied with what had just happened on the terrace that as he stopped at the end of the drive he didn't notice the suspicious-looking man dodging out of sight behind a hedge.

Eddie Sarno waited until the car was out of sight, then scurried across the road to the shelter of another group of trees. Then he ran down the road until he reached his car, which he had pulled into an unused, well-concealed road. Slipping behind the steering wheel, he flipped open a cooler which sat on the other side of the seat, took out a Coke and popped it open. Then he settled back to wait.

The digital figures on his watch said it was seven-fifteen. That meant he had about four hours to just think and listen to the birds. He liked birds. He didn't see a lot of them in the part of D.C. where he lived.

Sipping at the Coke, he let his mind run through the details of that night's job.

He had spent Thursday night and Friday casing the Ryan estate, and he knew the last person to leave the big barn was the lanky stable boy, Jeff. At about ten forty-five Jeff would take a last tour of all the stalls and the tack room, where all the expensive stuff they used on the horses was kept. Then he'd flip on the night light and take off to walk to his mobile home a good mile and a half across the back of the estate. It was far enough away so that he wouldn't come snooping back at the first scent of smoke.

That was when Eddie would go in, carrying

his two cans of gasoline, being sure to keep to the shadows, just in case anyone happened to be looking out of the house. Still, he'd be pretty safe there; there were a line of oaks and the tennis court fencing between him and the house.

He would work quickly—after all, he wasn't a pro for nothing. First he'd push some piles of hay up against the stalls, then a line of them across the door so no one could get in once the fire was burning. Then he'd sprinkle the gas around, set the low, stubby candles he always used in the center of each pile, and check to make sure the sprinkler system wasn't working. Finally, he'd touch his lighter to the wick of each candle and be off. The candles would give him about ten minutes get-away time. He'd be back at his car and on his way back to Washington to collect the rest of his money from that three-piece suit, Colin Wollman, before anyone in the big house had even thought to call the fire department.

He wished he had a better alibi, but his buddies would cover for him and say he had been playing poker with them all night. It would be a piece of cake, Eddie thought with a happy smile. He took another swallow of his soda and leaned his head back against the seat rest. Closing his eyes, he listened to the birds chirping to one another in a nearby tree.

# 15

Jed was bursting with frustration in the lobby of the New York airport. Apparently the entire world, or at least most of New York City, had decided to get out of the city at the same time. He had been stuck in traffic for hours and then his cab had broken down on the highway. Now it was getting late, and he had just missed a flight. He'd have to wait almost an hour for the next one.

It would be after eleven by the time he arrived at Ryan Acres. Caitlin would probably be getting ready for bed, and she wouldn't be too thrilled to see him at that hour. Not after the way he had acted on the phone earlier. Perhaps, he thought, it would be better to get an early flight the next morning. He could call her from Washington, apologize, and ask if they could have breakfast together.

Right, that was what he'd do, he decided, nodding to himself—take a plane to Washington on Sunday morning. Shifting the strap of his garment bag to a more comfortable position, he headed toward the outer door to the row of cabs that were lined up along the curb waiting for passengers.

After looking in on Melanie, Caitlin had gone into her own room. After changing out of her tennis things, she had showered and slipped into cotton slacks, a comfortable cotton sweater, and canvas flats.

Still upset about Howard's attitude toward Melanie, as well as Melanie's unhappiness and the phone conversation she had had with Jed, Caitlin discovered she was hungry. The last time she had eaten was at breakfast that morning. And that had only been toast and grapefruit juice. So much had happened that day, that she had completely forgotten about food. But now her stomach was positively growling. It was the two hours of hard tennis playing, she told herself as she went downstairs and headed for the kitchen.

She asked Mrs. Crowley to make up a couple of dinner trays, one for herself and a light one for Melanie. "Could you please ask Margaret to bring them upstairs?"

"Yes, miss." The middle-aged woman

nodded pleasantly. "Will there be anything else before I retire to my room, Miss Ryan?"

"No, thank you," Caitlin replied. "Have a nice night."

Caitlin decided to spend the rest of the evening in her room going over reports. Her bedroom was a more comfortable place to work than the library, and she really needed to relax. As she climbed back upstairs, she could feel the stiff tension in her neck. What a day it had been!

*Too bad Jed's not here*, she thought. He knew just how to rub her neck to loosen the tight muscles. *Jed*. Her mind went back to the argument they had had earlier. Why was it that right after something good happened—like Howard's finding out Colin was behind the rumors—something bad happened to cancel out the good? She shook her head.

Maybe a little something to eat would make her feel better. Then she would tackle those papers from the office. Concentrating on business for a few hours might be the best thing to get her mind off her other problems.

After he left Ryan Acres, Howard had driven aimlessly back toward Washington. He stopped at a coffee shop for a sandwich, but he had barely tasted it. There was too much on his mind. Caitlin was right, he had been too hard on Melanie. But he just couldn't help himself—she made him want to protect her.

He climbed back into his car and began driving again, cruising the lonely back country roads as his thoughts wandered.

What was wrong with him, anyway? Normally, he was very calm. He had to be so that he could deal with the pressures of his fast-paced job. Why, then, did Melanie Michaels always manage to set him off the way she did? Why, he asked himself, should he care about what she did with her life? If she really wanted to throw herself away on some no-good heel like Laurence Baxter, what business was it of his? Hell, he thought a moment later, mouth set in a grim line as he downshifted, it wasn't his business at all. Absolutely not. He stomped his foot down on the gas pedal, sending the car rocketing down the narrow, dark stretch of road in front of him.

Eddie had been crouching behind a stack of hay bales for some time, long enough so that his knees were beginning to hurt. It was almost time. Using a tiny flashlight, he checked his wrist for the time. It was ten fifty-five. Everything was on schedule so far. Jeff had been gone for almost ten minutes, and there wasn't a single light on at the back of the main house. There had only been lights on in those four windows on the second story in the front. Yeah, it was safe enough. Quietly he rose to his feet and made his way to the front doors of the stable. Once there, he quickly ducked inside.

The horses greeted him with soft nickers. He ignored them and quickly set to work, pulling bales of hay together. He set the unlit candles in the center of pieces of thick paper so that once they burned down, the gasoline soaked hay would easily catch. Everything would burn fast—and completely, leaving not a trace of evidence.

Up in her room, Caitlin had just finished reading the same paragraph for the third time. Realizing that she didn't remember a single word of what she had just read, she threw the paper down. Standing up, she began walking restlessly around the room. She ran a finger along the edge of her dresser, picked up and then put down a small jade figurine that was sitting on the table by the chaise. Pausing by her bed, she reached down and picked up a framed photograph of Jed. It was in a folding leather case, the one she always took with her whenever she traveled.

Holding it in her hands, she looked at Jed's face—it was so strong and so terribly handsome. She loved him very much, but sometimes he just didn't understand her needs. Why couldn't he see that she had to keep her promise to herself about finishing the projects at Ryan Mining? But, no, he wanted her to just hurry up and sell the company, without any thought for the people who worked for Ryan Mining. He kept telling her that she'd made a great start and that any well-meaning owner would carry on and continue her work. But would that really happen? She didn't know. Caitlin's eyes had finally been opened to a responsibility that had been there all along, something she had refused to see before—her responsibility to her grandmother and to the Ryan legacy.

Tenderly, Caitlin set the photo down again. She had other worries as well—whatever was going on between Howard and Melanie, Melanie's pain because of Laurence—

She let out a sad laugh. At that moment the only uncomplicated relationship in her life was the one with her horses. Perhaps she would go down to the stable and say good night to Duster and the newcomers, King and Sunshine. Yes, that's just what she'd do. Going over to the dresser, she took out a light sweater, threw it over her shoulders, and left the room.

It took Eddie longer than he had thought it would to arrange all the piles of hay. The stable was larger than he had first thought.

But finally he was finished, and he began lighting the candles. He was just inside the front doors, having worked his way down one long aisle. Suddenly he heard a noise. Stopping short, he listened.

Someone had just entered the barn. *Could Jeff have come back for some reason?* he wondered. Moving to the corner, he peered around it and into the short cross aisle that formed the entry. It was still dark there. He strained his eyes, trying to see who was there. But all he could make out was a figure.

Quickly, he went back to pinch out the candles. He could always light them again later, after the person had gone. But to his horror, he saw that the fire had already started and was beginning to spread. *Damn*, he thought, he must have spilled some of the gasoline near a candle. Either that or one of the candles had accidentally tipped over.

He was trapped! There was no way out, except past the person who stood between him and the front door. Panicking, he began trying to stamp out the fire. But it was too far gone. It was everywhere. And the smoke was getting to him—choking him—his eyes hurt—he couldn't breathe—and, his pant leg was on fire. He beat at it.

Whirling about, he ran for the doors. She was there—a girl dressed in white—over by the wall. Who the hell was she?

He saw her eyes widen in fear.

He hit her, pausing long enough to see her collapse down onto the ground. Then he shut the doors and was gone outside into the darkness. His leg hurt so much that he wanted to limp, but he forced himself to run hard. Finally, gasping for breath, he reached his car and threw himself in. Shaking, he forced the keys into the ignition.

Melanie was not packing neatly. All five pieces of her pale blue luggage sat on the floor, open. Taking clothes from the closet and the drawers of the two dressers, she dropped them into whichever case was nearest. She no longer felt as devastated as she had earlier. She had done some serious thinking.

Laurence really was a rat, she saw that now. In fact, he was more than a rat—he was a lowlife. Pitching a shoe into a nearby bag, she vowed she never wanted to see him again. That was why she wanted to go back to New York. She certainly didn't want to leave Caitlin—or Ryan Acres. She had begun to feel really at home there. In a way, it was almost like being back on the ranch in Montana, open countryside and hills and, of course, the horses. There weren't any horses or hills back in New York. Well, she told herself, dropping some dresses into one of the larger suitcases, she'd just have to live with her decision. She couldn't back down now.

Turning around, Melanie started toward the closet again. But then she stopped—she thought she smelled smoke. Yes, it *was* smoke, and it was coming through the window she had left open. Crossing to the window, she sniffed again. The smell was even stronger.

Then suddenly a horrible sound cut through the night silence—a terrible, screeching whinny of terror.

Something was dreadfully wrong. Racing from the room, Melanie called, "Caitlin—Caitlin!"

She pounded on Caitlin's door, but there was no answer. She opened the door and looked in the room. It was empty.

She heard another agonizing whinny, this time through Caitlin's window.

Leaving the room, she raced down the stairs and rushed through the house, continuing to call Caitlin's name. There was no answer.

Where was she?

Reaching the library, she ran to the french doors and threw them open. Now she could see flames coming from the stable, tongues of fire darkened by the billowing smoke leaped upward toward the stars.

*Caitlin must have gone to the barn.* It was the only answer! She must get help. Melanie's mind worked clearly, although her body was shaking as she ran to the servant's wing. "Rollins! Margaret! Get everyone up, there's a fire!"

She told Rollins to call the fire department. Then to gather the rest of the staff and hurry to the stable. She ran back through the house and out the french doors. As fast as she could, she took off in the direction of the burning stable.

Just as Melanie was racing across the back lawn, Howard drove up in front to Ryan Acres, somewhat surprised to find that he'd driven there. He hadn't meant to go anywhere in particular. And yet, there he was, back where he had started from. Perhaps it was fate, he thought. Or more likely, his conscience was bothering him and he came back to Ryan Acres to apologize to Caitlin for his boorish behavior.

It was late, he knew, but he could at least drive up the long driveway, to see if there were any lights on downstairs. If there were, it would mean that Caitlin was still up.

As he pulled up in front of the house he could smell smoke. Searching the scene, he noticed flames coming from the direction of the stable. Taking the front steps three at a time, he rushed up to the front door and banged on it. Margaret finally opened the door. She and Mrs. Crowley, both in bathrobes, were standing there, wringing their hands, their eyes wide with fright.

"Where's Caitlin?" he yelled.

"We're not sure, maybe in the barn," Margaret said.

In an instant he raced down the long marble hall, dodging into the library, then out the same doors Melanie had gone through minutes earlier.

Arriving at the stable, Melanie found the doors shut with smoke pouring out beneath them. Now positive that Caitlin must be inside, she pulled the doors open. Smoke billowed out and the sounds which greeted her were horrifying—the crackle of flames and the screams of terrified horses.

As Howard came up behind her she also saw the staff who had come racing to the stables. "Quick," she called, "the horses must be saved. Get something to serve as blindfolds. You'll have to lead them out individually. The won't leave their stalls otherwise."

"I don't know anything about horses," Howard admitted in a breathless voice. "How can I help?"

"I think Caitlin is in there!" Melanie screamed, her voice shaking with fright. "Please, please help me save her!"

Howard pulled out the handkerchief he had let her use earlier, dipped it in a nearby rain barrel, and handed it to her. "Put this over your mouth. It'll help you breathe."

Her eyes questioned him, but there wasn't time to argue. Together they fought their way in through the smoke. About twenty feet in Melanie spotted a crumpled white figure lying next to a wall—Caitlin. She started to call to Howard, but realized that trying to speak was impossible.

Howard had seen her and was starting toward her to help her from the other side of the aisle. Just then one of the horses, a powerful bay gelding that was being led from the stable shied as Howard stepped into his path. The horse reared and came slashing down, one hoof striking the attorney and sending him crashing into the same wall against which Caitlin was huddled.

Howard! Melanie wanted to scream, but she didn't. He appeared to be unconscious. She wanted to go to him, but first there was Caitlin. Melanie didn't know how long Caitlin had been inhaling smoke—she had to get her outside immediately.

Anxious about Howard, she took the damp handkerchief from her mouth, leaned down, and laid it over his mouth. Then, grabbing Caitlin's shoulders she pulled her from the building. As the fresh air hit Caitlin's face, she began to revive. She coughed at first, trying to catch her breath. Then, suddenly, Jed appeared. He put his arms about her, holding her.

"Jed!" she said, her voice barely audible. It was hoarse from the smoke. "What—what happened? Wh-what are you doing here? How—"

"Never mind that now," Melanie interrupted urgently. Anxiously she grabbed at Jed's arm. "You've got to help me. Howard's inside, and he's hurt. Jed!"

"Go!" Caitlin urged him.

With a quick nod, Jed stood and ran toward the barn, following Melanie, who had already rushed back into the burning building.

Melanie reached Howard first. She was kneeling by his side when Jed got there.

The smoke was still thick and talking was impossible. Howard was only semiconscious. It was obvious to Jed that he would have to be carried. But he must weigh one hundred and eighty pounds, and it would be almost impossible for Jed to carry him. Not only that, Howard's leg was bent at such an angle that Jed was almost certain it was broken.

Melanie looked at him frantically, her eyes pleading with him to do something.

Then he remembered the cross-handed carry he had learned in a Red Cross class. Melanie had taken the same class, too. Pantomiming what he wanted to do, he saw she understood. There was a look of relief on her smoke-smudged face as she put her hands out to cross with his.

A minute later the three of them emerged from the barn, Howard being carried easily between Melanie and Jed. They continued on across the yard to where Caitlin was now leaning against a tree. Gently, they set him down. He had regained consciousness and winced as his injured leg touched the ground.

Melanie once more knelt beside him. With a light touch, she stroked his shoulder. "Oh, Howard, I'm so glad you're safe. I was so terrified when you were trapped in there." Tears of happiness slid down her cheeks.

"You were—you were really worried?" Howard asked quietly, his eyes looking directly into hers.

"Yes. Yes, I was," she whispered, nodding. And as he wiped away her tears, a look of complete and new understanding passed between them. But the spell was broken by Caitlin's concerned voice. "What about the horses? Are they out? Duster? King? Sunshine?"

"The stable hands and the others were getting them out," Jed replied immediately. "But I'll go check." Turning around, he started toward the tangle of horses and men milling about in the stable yard.

When Jed came back to them, he nodded to Caitlin.

"Well?" Caitlin's voice was anxious.

"They're safe. All of them," Jed reported.

"Three of the brood mares might have some slight burns. But Jeff doesn't believe they're anything to worry about. The vet has already been called and is coming right out."

"Was anyone hurt?" Howard wanted to know.

"Two of the men had some injuries. Not bad, though," he said, reassuring them. "One a sprained wrist, another got some cuts and bruises when a burning two-by-four fell on his arms."

"Thank God it wasn't anything serious," Caitlin said, relieved.

"I told the men to put the horses into the small paddocks until the vet gets here and checks them out."

"What about Howard—and the other men?" Melanie asked. "Did you call an ambulance?"

"The paramedics are on their way, along with the fire department." He paused, listening for the sirens in the distance. "Which is almost here," he said, angry at how long it had taken them.

With a faint smile, Caitlin reached out and touched Jed's hand. "This is the country, remember?"

"Yeah, I guess you're right," Jed replied with the hint of a wry smile showing at the corners of his mouth. "It isn't like New York, is it?"

Caitlin shook her head. "No, it's—home," she barely whispered.

"I know," Jed said in a low voice. "I know that now, too." Slipping his arm around Caitlin's shoulders, he held her close as they watched the rest of the stable burn. All that the firefighters could do was to contain the flames as they burned themselves out.

When the ambulance arrived, Melanie insisted she be allowed to ride to the hospital with Howard. As they sped through the night, he thought of how lucky he was—and how truly lovely the girl who sat beside him was. Her face was smeared with soot, her clothes were absolutely ruined, and there was bandage on her arm where she had been burned as she and Jed had helped him from the stable. But she was still beautiful. And in that moment of life and death when he had seen her act without any thought to her own safety, risking her life to save his life and Caitlin's, he had realized just how wonderful a person she really was. And when he had looked into her eyes afterward, feeling even more strongly the emotion that had passed between them, he knew why he had cared so much about her relationship with Laurence. It was because he loved her. It was as simple as that.

# 16

The warm sun beat down on her shoulders. A light breeze was blowing across the pasture, bringing with it the smell of timothy and clover and August flowers. Caitlin was positive she had never been happier.

She and Jed were leaning against the top rail of one of the side pastures, watching the horses. Sunshine looked as if she were playing hide-and-seek with King. First she'd gallop to one end of the enclosed meadow, slip behind one of the other horses, then peek out. She'd nicker to get his attention, then dash off again with a mischievous little kick of her heels.

"She's an outright flirt, isn't she?" Jed remarked with a smile.

"She's just pretty and she knows it," Caitlin

said as she turned to him with a twinkle in her deep blue eyes.

"Oh, really? You used to be a terrific flirt, too," Jed said. "If I remember right."

"I suppose I was." Caitlin tipped her head to one side as her lips curved into a lovely smile. "But now it's only you. There's never going to be another man in my life—ever." She punched his shoulder playfully. "Sorry, mister, but that's the way it goes."

"No chance of getting out of our wedding plans, huh?"

"Absolutely not!" she assured him. "Three weeks from now, you are going to tell the world that you will love and cherish me—until death do us part."

"Then why don't we just leave it out of the ceremony," Jed suggested. "And replace it with forever."

"Forever it is," she said happily.

She was silent for a moment, looking back at the horses. Beyond them, the foundation for the new stable was already being laid. There would be improvements over the old one, all the latest in monitoring equipment, with TV-tracking cameras covering the stall areas to prevent a disaster from ever happening again.

Caitlin put her hand on Jed's arm, rubbing her thumb along the warm flesh. "Jed?"

"Yes?" He turned to her again.

"You are happy with your decision, aren't you?" There was a tiny touch of worry in her voice.

"You mean to leave New York and go into the horse-breeding business?" He nodded. "Yes, I'm really happy about it." He shifted his weight slightly so that he could slide his arm around her waist and pull her against him. "You know it's scary to think about how close I came to not making it down here last Saturday night. I had missed those flights, and I was just about to walk out of the terminal and grab a cab back to my apartment, when I thought I heard you calling me. That's when I turned back." He shook his head. "I don't know. I never believed in that sort of thing, but now I think I do. It's like people who love each other have some kind of—telepathy."

Caitlin nodded. "Well, I don't think I knew I was going to be in danger then, but I do know I was thinking about you." Her voice softened. "I knew I needed you and wanted you. And I think maybe I was trying to send a message to you saying how much you meant to me."

He held her even closer. "And I promise I will always be there for you. I'll never let anything hurt you ever again. I promise."

"Well, I'm just glad that they caught that

man who set the fire." She couldn't finish the rest.

"It's lucky he implicated Colin, too." Jed nodded. "I guess we can be sure that Mr. Wollman will be locked up for good this time."

She nodded, burying her face against his shoulder.

"That fire was a terrible thing," Jed said softly. "But something good did come out of it. I realized that I didn't have my priorities straight."

She raised her head to look up at his face and saw in his expression just how deeply he loved her.

"I realized," he went on, "that everything that's important to me is right here at Ryan Acres. This is where my life is—with you, my love. And working together we'll be the best." He smiled down at her. "Ryan Acres and Ryan Mining. We'll be unbeatable."

"Unbeatable," she repeated lovingly, as she put her head back against his shoulder. "Forever and always."

## FRANCINE PASCAL

In addition to collaborating on the Broadway musical *George M!* and the nonfiction book *The Strange Case of Patty Hearst*, Francine Pascal has written an adult novel, *Save Johanna!*, and four young adult novels, *Hangin' Out with Cici*, *My First Love and Other Disasters*, *The Hand-Me-Down Kid*, and *Love and Betrayal & Hold the Mayo!* She is also the creator of the Sweet Valley High and Sweet Valley Twins series. Ms. Pascal has three daughters, Jamie, Susan, and Laurie, and lives in New York City.

## DIANA GREGORY

Growing up in Hollywood, Diana Gregory wanted to become an actress. She became an associate TV producer instead. Now a full-time writer, she has written, in addition to other books, three young adult novels, *I'm Boo! That's Who!*, *There's a Caterpillar in My Lemonade*, and *The Fog Burns Off by Eleven O'clock*, plus several Sweet Dreams novels. Besides writing, her other love is traveling. She has lived in several states, including Virginia, where she stayed on a horse farm for a year. She now calls Seattle home.